Texas STAAR Grade 7 Math Made Easy

Study Guide with Key Concepts, Review & Practice

Dr. A. Nazari

Published by View Math Education
ViewMath.com

ViewMath.com/TX-Grade7

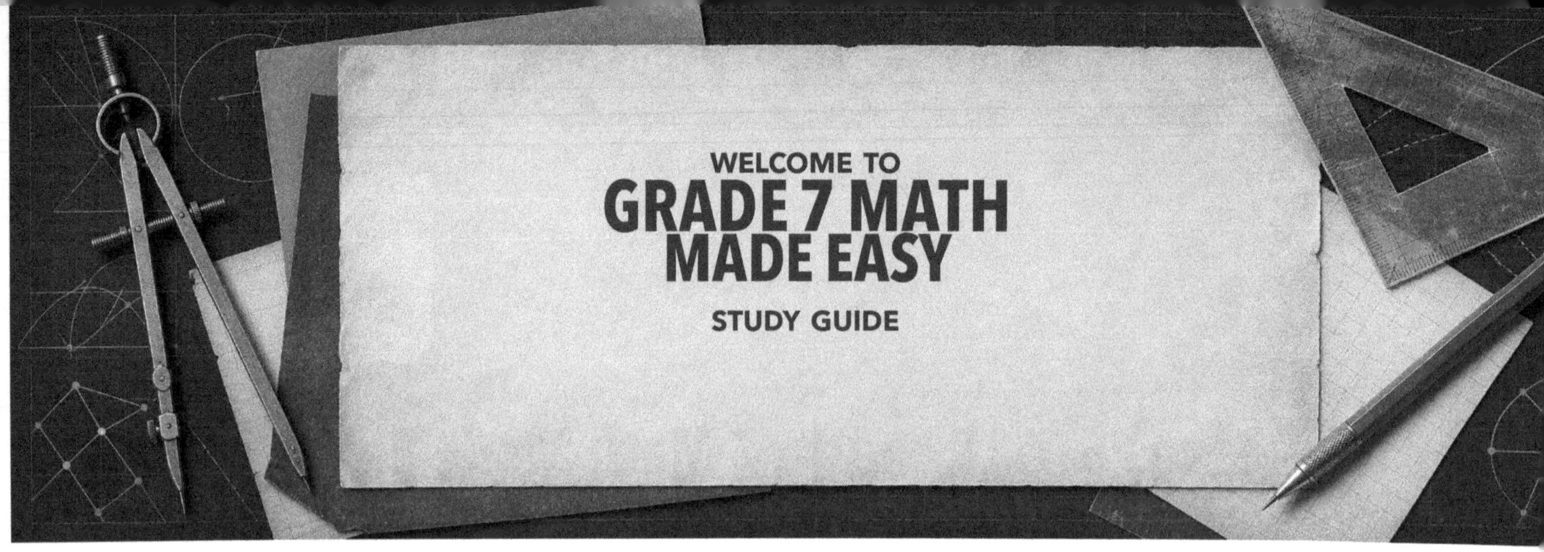

Build a method you can explain, check, and use again.

Grade 7 mathematics links proportional reasoning, rational-number operations, algebra, geometry, statistics, and probability. This guide makes those connections explicit: each topic begins with the central idea, develops it through worked examples, and then asks you to apply it without relying on the model.

See the structure

- connect tables, graphs, equations, and verbal rules
- identify which quantities and operations control a problem
- recognize when two methods express the same relationship
- separate a useful rule from a memorized shortcut

Work with precision

- record enough reasoning to locate an error
- estimate first, then test whether the exact answer is reasonable
- use units, labels, and scale consistently
- correct the method before attempting a similar problem

A focused study rhythm. Read one concept, reconstruct the example, practice without looking back, and check the explanation—not only the final answer.

HOW TO USE THIS BOOK

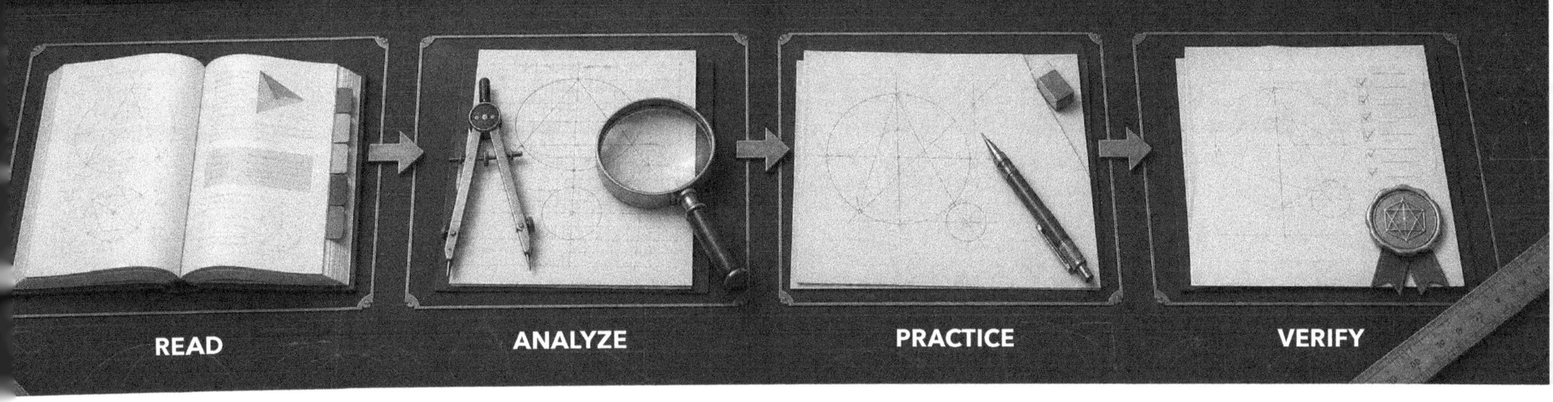

Treat every section as a cycle: understand the idea, test the method, and use the correction as the next lesson.

Worked examples are models, not scripts to copy. Decide why each step is valid and whether the same reasoning applies when the numbers, representation, or context changes.

Read the concept Identify the quantities, relationship, rule, and unit. State the central idea in your own words before moving to the example.

Analyze the example Recreate each line. Ask what changed, which property justified the change, and how the result was checked.

Practice independently Hide the model and solve with visible reasoning. Estimate when possible and keep units attached.

Verify the method Compare with the answer explanation. Classify a miss as a concept, setup, calculation, notation, or checking error.

Transfer the learning Correct the work, then solve one related problem without notes. A corrected answer matters when the method also changes.

20-30 MINUTES SHOW THE REASONING RETEST MISSES

MATH QUICK REFERENCE

MADE EASY • CORE RELATIONSHIPS, RULES, AND FORMULAS

Recall the relationship first. Use this page to confirm notation, units, and the order of operations.

Proportional relationships

$y = kx$, where $k = \frac{y}{x}$.

The constant k is the unit rate. A proportional graph is a straight line through the origin.

Percent problems

part = percent × whole

Percent change: $\frac{|\text{new} - \text{original}|}{|\text{original}|} \times 100\%$

Simple interest: $I = Prt$

Rational-number operations

Add: same signs–add and keep the sign; different signs–subtract absolute values and keep the sign of the greater absolute value.

Subtract: add the opposite.

Multiply/divide: same signs give $+$; different signs give $-$.

Expressions and equations

Distributive property: $a(b + c) = ab + ac$

For $ax + b = c$, subtract b, then divide by a. Check by substitution.

Inequalities

Solve as an equation, but reverse the inequality when multiplying or dividing by a negative number.

$x > 3$: open circle; $x \geq 3$: closed circle.

Geometry and scale

Scale factor: $\frac{\text{drawing length}}{\text{actual length}}$

Supplementary angles sum to $180°$; complementary angles sum to $90°$; vertical angles are congruent.

Circles, area, and volume

$C = 2\pi r = \pi d$ $A_{\text{circle}} = \pi r^2$

$A_{\triangle} = \frac{1}{2}bh$ $V_{\text{prism}} = Bh$

Square area units and cube volume units.

Probability and statistics

$P(\text{event}) = \frac{\text{favorable outcomes}}{\text{total outcomes}}$, with $0 \leq P \leq 1$.

Organize compound-event sample spaces with a tree, table, or systematic list.

CONTENTS

A clear route from proportional reasoning to probability.

Use the chapters in order for a complete review, or move directly to the topic you need and return to the answer explanations afterward.

9 CHAPTERS • WORKED EXAMPLES • PRACTICE WITH ANSWERS

CHAPTER

1

Ratios and Proportional Relationships

What's Inside

1.1 Unit Rates with Fractions

Learning Goals

- Compute unit rates when quantities are fractions
- Compare rates by finding unit rates

Unit Rates with Fractions

A **unit rate** tells you how much of one quantity per **one unit** of another. When the quantities are fractions, divide just like before:

$$\text{unit rate} = \frac{\text{first quantity}}{\text{second quantity}}$$

To divide fractions, **multiply by the reciprocal** (Keep–Change–Flip):

$$\frac{a}{b} \div \frac{c}{d} = \frac{a}{b} \times \frac{d}{c}$$

Finding a Unit Rate

A recipe uses $\frac{3}{4}$ cup of sugar for $\frac{1}{2}$ batch. How much sugar per batch?

Solution:

$$\frac{3}{4} \div \frac{1}{2} = \frac{3}{4} \times \frac{2}{1} = \frac{6}{4} = \frac{3}{2}$$

Answer: $1\frac{1}{2}$ **cups per batch**

Comparing Two Rates

Who walks faster?

- Ana: $\frac{2}{3}$ mi in $\frac{1}{4}$ hr
- Ben: $\frac{3}{4}$ mi in $\frac{1}{3}$ hr

Ana: $\frac{2}{3} \div \frac{1}{4} = \frac{8}{3} = 2\frac{2}{3}$ mph

Ben: $\frac{3}{4} \div \frac{1}{3} = \frac{9}{4} = 2\frac{1}{4}$ mph

$2\frac{2}{3} > 2\frac{1}{4}$ ⊠ **Ana is faster.**

> *"Per" means "for every one." To find a unit rate, always divide!*

Unit Rates with Fractions

1. A painter covers $\frac{2}{3}$ of a wall in $\frac{1}{3}$ hour. How much wall per hour?
2. A faucet leaks $\frac{1}{2}$ cup in $\frac{3}{4}$ minute. How many cups per minute?
3. A car uses $\frac{5}{6}$ gallon to travel $\frac{2}{3}$ mile. How many gallons per mile?
4. Trail mix A: $\frac{1}{2}$ cup nuts for $\frac{1}{4}$ cup raisins. Trail mix B: $\frac{2}{3}$ cup nuts for $\frac{1}{3}$ cup raisins. Which has more nuts per cup of raisins?
5. A snail crawls $\frac{5}{8}$ m in $\frac{3}{4}$ hr. A beetle crawls $\frac{7}{10}$ m in $\frac{4}{5}$ hr. Which is faster?

1.2 Recognizing Proportional Relationships

Learning Goals

- Decide whether two quantities are proportional using a table or graph
- Explain why a relationship is or is not proportional

What Makes It Proportional?

Two quantities are **proportional** if every pair has the **same ratio**.

- **Table test:** Divide $y \div x$ for every row. Same quotient every time $=$ proportional.
- **Graph test:** Points form a **straight line through the origin** $(0, 0)$.

One mismatch means not proportional.

Table Test

Hours (x)	Pay (y)	$y \div x$
2	\$24	12
5	\$60	12
8	\$96	12

Every ratio is 12 ⊠ **proportional** at \$12/hr. Now add a \$20 sign-up fee: costs become \$44, \$80, \$116. Ratios: $22, 16, 14.5$ ⊠ **not proportional**.

Just a Straight Line?

"The graph is a straight line, so it must be proportional." **Not quite!** The line must also pass through $(0,0)$. A line crossing the y-axis at 5 is not proportional.

> *No sign-up fees, no starting amounts. Proportional means it starts at zero and stays straight!*

Recognizing Proportional Relationships

1. Is this relationship proportional? Explain.

x	y
3	9
5	15
7	21

2. Is this relationship proportional? Explain.

x	y
2	6
4	10
6	14

3. A straight line through $(0,0)$ always shows a proportional relationship. **True** ○ **False** ○

4. A phone plan costs $\$0.05$ per text with no monthly fee. A second plan costs $\$5$/month plus $\$0.02$ per text. Which is proportional?

1.3 Finding the Constant of Proportionality

Learning Goals

- Find the constant of proportionality (k) from tables, graphs, and descriptions
- Understand that k equals the unit rate

The Constant of Proportionality

In a proportional relationship, every ratio $\frac{y}{x}$ equals the same value called k:

$$k = \frac{y}{x}$$

k is the **unit rate** — how much y changes for every 1 unit of x.

- **From a table:** divide any y by its x.
- **From a graph:** read the y-value at $x = 1$, or pick any point and compute $\frac{y}{x}$.
- **From words:** divide the two quantities.

Finding k from a Table

Apples cost a fixed price per pound.

Pounds (x)	Cost (y)
2	\$3.50
4	\$7.00
6	\$10.50

$k = \frac{3.50}{2} = 1.75$. Check: $\frac{7.00}{4} = 1.75$ ✓

Answer: $k = 1.75$ ⊠ **apples cost $\$1.75$ per pound.**

> *"k, unit rate, rate of change — they all mean the same thing. Always include* ***units*** *when you state k!"*

Finding the Constant of Proportionality

1. Find k.

x	y
3	12
5	20
8	32

2. Find k and explain what it means.

Hours	Miles
$\frac{1}{2}$	30
1	60
2	120

3. A proportional graph passes through $(6, 15)$. Find k.

4. A printer prints 80 pages in 5 minutes at a constant rate. What is k?

5. The table shows a proportional relationship. Find the missing value.

x	y
4	14
6	?
10	35

1.4 Writing Equations for Proportional Relationships

Learning Goals

- Write equations of the form $y = kx$ for proportional relationships
- Use equations to find unknown values

The Proportional Equation

Every proportional relationship can be written as:

$$y = kx$$

Find k (the unit rate), then write the equation.

Situation	Equation
Oranges cost $0.75 each	$c = 0.75n$
A car goes 60 mph	$d = 60t$
Earn $12 per hour	$p = 12h$

Once you know k, you can predict y for ANY value of x.

From a Table to an Equation

A farmer sells strawberries at a constant price.

Pounds (x)	Cost (y)
3	$13.50
5	$22.50

$k = 13.50 \div 3 = 4.50$, so the equation is $c = 4.50p$. For 8 pounds: $c = 4.50 \times 8 = \$36$.

Answer: $c = 4.50p$

> *An equation is a prediction machine. Plug in any x, and out comes the matching y!*

Writing Equations

1. A bike rental costs $8 per hour. Write an equation for total cost c in terms of hours h.
2. Water flows at 3.5 gallons per minute. Write an equation for gallons g in terms of minutes m.
3. Use the table to write an equation.

x	y
4	10
6	15
10	25

4. A recipe uses $\frac{3}{4}$ cup of flour per serving. How much flour for 12 servings?
5. A cell phone plan charges $0.04 per text. You have $10. How many texts can you send?

★ 1.5 Graphing Proportional Relationships ★

Learning Goals

- Explain what $(0,0)$ and $(1,r)$ mean on a proportional graph
- Connect the steepness of a line to the unit rate

Graphing $y = kx$

A proportional relationship graphs as a **straight line through** $(0,0)$. Two special points:

- $(0,0)$: zero of one gives zero of the other.
- $(1,r)$: the y-value at $x = 1$ IS the unit rate.

Steeper line = greater unit rate. This steepness is called the **slope**, and slope $= k$.

Graphing from a Table

A car uses gas at a constant rate.

Gallons (x)	Miles (y)
0	0
1	30
2	60
4	120

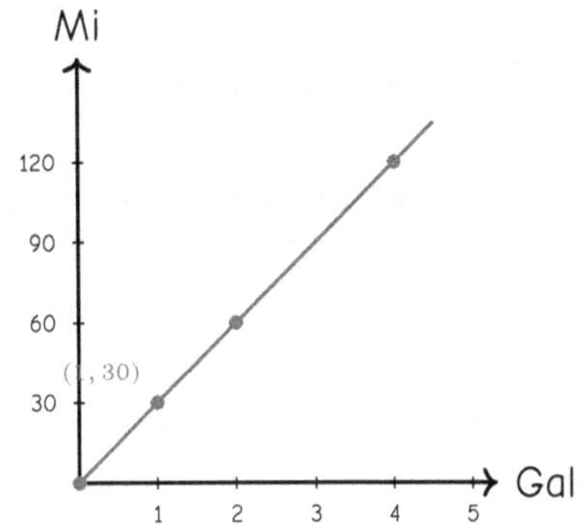

$(1, 30)$ ⊠ unit rate is 30 miles per gallon.

To compare rates, graph both on the same axes. The steeper line wins!

Graphing Proportional Relationships

1. The equation $y = 5x$ gives the cost of movie tickets. What does $(1, 5)$ mean?
2. A proportional graph passes through $(3, 18)$. Find the unit rate and y when $x = 7$.
3. Runner A: $(2, 10)$. Runner B: $(2, 8)$. Both start at $(0, 0)$. Who is faster?
4. A steeper line on a proportional graph means a smaller unit rate. True ◯ False ◯
5. A graph passes through $(5, 12.5)$. Write the equation and find x when $y = 40$.

1.6 Applying Proportional Reasoning

Learning Goals

- Solve real-world proportion problems using the best strategy
- Choose between unit rate, proportion, or equation approaches

Your Proportional Reasoning Toolbox

1. **Unit rate** — find the rate for 1 unit, then multiply
2. **Proportion** — set up $\frac{a}{b} = \frac{c}{d}$ and cross-multiply
3. **Equation** — use $y = kx$
4. **Scale factor** — multiply or divide to scale up/down

Pick whichever feels most natural. They all give the same answer.

Unit Rate Strategy

5 T-shirts cost \$42.50. How much for 8?

Solution:

$\$42.50 \div 5 = \$8.50$ per shirt. $\$8.50 \times 8 = \$68$.

Answer: $\$68.00$

Proportion Strategy

A map scale: 2 cm $=15$ mi. Two cities are 7 cm apart. Actual distance?

Solution:

$\frac{2}{15}=\frac{7}{d}$ ⊠ $2d=105$ ⊠ $d=52.5$ miles.

Answer: 52.5 **miles**

> *Not sure which strategy? Try the unit rate first — it works for almost everything!*

TIP

After solving, ask: does the answer make sense? Buying MORE should cost MORE. Always check your units.

Applying Proportional Reasoning

1. A car travels 210 miles on 6 gallons. How far on 10 gallons?
2. A recipe for 4 people uses $\frac{3}{2}$ cups of rice. How much for 10 people?
3. On a map, 3 cm $=24$ km. How many km is 8 cm?
4. A printer prints 120 pages in 8 min. How long for 450 pages?
5. Small paint: $\frac{3}{4}$ gal for \$18. Large: $1\frac{1}{2}$ gal for \$33. Which is the better deal?

CHAPTER

2

Percents in Everyday Life

What's Inside

2.1 Solving Percent Problems

Learning Goals

- Find a percent of a number, the whole, or the percent
- Solve percent problems using equations and proportions

Three Types of Percent Problems

Every percent problem has three parts: the **part**, the **whole**, and the **percent**.

$$\text{part} = \text{percent} \times \text{whole}$$

- **Find the part:** What is 30% of 80? ⊠ $0.30 \times 80 = 24$
- **Find the whole:** 15 is 25% of what? ⊠ $15 \div 0.25 = 60$
- **Find the percent:** 12 is what percent of 48? ⊠ $12 \div 48 = 0.25 = 25\%$

Using a Proportion

18 is 40% of what number?

Set up a proportion: $\dfrac{18}{w} = \dfrac{40}{100}$

Cross-multiply: $18 \times 100 = 40 \times w$ ⊠ $1800 = 40w$ ⊠ $w = 45$

Answer: The whole is 45.

> "Is" means equals. "Of" means multiply. So "20% of 50" becomes 0.20×50.

Solving Percent Problems

1. What is 15% of 200?
2. 36 is what percent of 90?
3. 27 is 75% of what number?
4. A student got 42 out of 60 questions right. What percent is that?
5. A store has 240 items. If 85% are in stock, how many are in stock?

2.2 Connecting Percents and Proportions

Learning Goals

- Set up proportions to solve percent problems
- Understand that percent is a ratio with denominator 100

Percent as a Proportion

"Percent" means "per hundred." Every percent problem is a proportion:

$$\frac{\text{part}}{\text{whole}} = \frac{\text{percent}}{100}$$

To solve, **cross-multiply** and divide.

Setting Up the Proportion

A survey found that 33 out of 150 students ride the bus. What percent is that?

$\frac{33}{150} = \frac{p}{100}$ ⊠ $33 \times 100 = 150 \times p$ ⊠ $3300 = 150p$ ⊠ $p = 22$

Answer: 22% **of students ride the bus.**

Choosing the Method

65% of a class of 40 earned an A. How many students earned an A?

Proportion: $\frac{n}{40} = \frac{65}{100}$
$100n = 2600$ ⊠ $n = 26$

Equation: $n = 0.65 \times 40 = 26$ ✓

Both methods give the same answer.

TIP

The proportion method works every time: put the part over the whole on the left, and the percent over 100 on the right. Cross-multiply to solve.

Connecting Percents and Proportions

1. Set up a proportion and solve: What is 45% of 80?
2. 54 is what percent of 120? Use a proportion.
3. 78 is 60% of what number?
4. In a bag of 250 marbles, 35 are red. What percent are red?
5. A school has 480 students. If 72% brought lunch, how many brought lunch?

★ 2.3 Percent Increase and Decrease ★

Learning Goals

- Calculate percent increase and percent decrease
- Use multipliers like 1.05 and 0.80 for quick calculations

Percent Change

Percent increase and **percent decrease** describe how much a value changes compared to the original.

$$\text{percent change} = \frac{|\text{new} - \text{original}|}{\text{original}} \times 100$$

Shortcut with multipliers:

- Increase by 5%: multiply by $1 + 0.05 = 1.05$
- Decrease by 20%: multiply by $1 - 0.20 = 0.80$

Using the Multiplier

A jacket was $\$60$. The price increased by 15%. What is the new price?

Multiplier: $1 + 0.15 = 1.15$

New price: $60 \times 1.15 = 69$

Answer: The new price is $\$69$.

Common Mistake

~~A $50 item is on sale for 30% off. New price: $50 \times 0.30 = \$15$.~~ $\longrightarrow$ ____________

0.30 gives the **discount amount**, not the sale price. Correct: $50 \times 0.70 = \$35$ or $50 - 15 = \$35$.

Percent Increase and Decrease

1. A town's population grew from 8,000 to 9,200. Find the percent increase.
2. A bike was $180. It is now 25% off. What is the sale price?
3. A plant was 12 cm tall. It grew to 15 cm. Find the percent increase.
4. What multiplier gives a 40% decrease?
5. A video game's price dropped from $40 to $32. Find the percent decrease.

2.4 Markups, Discounts, and Sales Tax

Learning Goals

- Calculate markups, discounts, and sales tax
- Find the final price after multiple percent changes

Markups and Discounts

- A **markup** is the amount a store adds to the cost. If a store pays $\$20$ and marks up 50%: selling price $= 20 \times 1.50 = \$30$.
- A **discount** is the amount subtracted from the price. A $\$30$ item at 20% off: sale price $= 30 \times 0.80 = \$24$.
- **Sales tax** is added to the price at checkout. If tax is 8%: total $=$ price $\times 1.08$.

Finding a Final Price

A store buys a shirt for $\$15$ and marks it up 60%. A customer buys it during a 25% off sale. Sales tax is 7%. What is the final price?

Step 1: Markup: $15 \times 1.60 = \$24$

Step 2: Discount: $24 \times 0.75 = \$18$

Step 3: Tax: $18 \times 1.07 = \$19.26$

Answer: **The final price is** $\$19.26$.

> *Apply markup first, then discount, then tax. Tax is always applied* ***last****, on the price the customer actually pays.*

Markups, Discounts, and Sales Tax

1. A store buys headphones for $12 and marks them up 75%. What is the selling price?
2. A $65 jacket is 30% off. What is the sale price?
3. A meal costs $22. Sales tax is 6%. What is the total?
4. Shoes cost $80, discount 15%, tax 8%. Find the final price.
5. A store buys a game for $25 and sells it for $40. What is the percent markup?

2.5 Tips, Commissions, and Fees

Learning Goals

- Calculate tips, commissions, and fees using percents
- Estimate tips mentally using benchmarks

Percent in Everyday Money

- A **tip** (gratuity) is extra money you pay for service. Common tips: 15%–20%.
- A **commission** is a percent of the total sales a worker earns. A realtor earning 3% commission on a \$200,000 sale gets \$6,000.
- A **fee** is a flat or percent charge for a service, like a 2.5% transaction fee.

Quick Tip Estimation

Your restaurant bill is \$47.80. Estimate a 20% tip.

Round to \$48. Find 10%: \$4.80. Double it: \$9.60.

Answer: A 20% tip is about \$9.60.

TIP
To estimate any tip: find 10% by moving the decimal one place left. For 15%, add half of 10%. For 20%, double the 10%.

Tips, Commissions, and Fees

1. A dinner bill is $35. You leave a 18% tip. How much is the tip?
2. A salesperson earns 6% commission. She sells $4,500 worth of electronics. What is her commission?
3. A ticket website charges a 12% service fee. Tickets cost $75. What is the total?
4. Estimate a 15% tip on a $62 bill using the 10% method.
5. A real estate agent earns 4% commission on a $350,000 house. How much does she earn?

2.6 Simple Interest: Earning and Paying Interest

Learning Goals

- Use $I = Prt$ to calculate simple interest for savings and loans
- Compare financial options using interest calculations

The Simple Interest Formula

Simple interest is money earned on savings or owed on loans.

$$I = Prt$$

- I = interest (dollars earned or owed)
- P = principal (starting amount)
- r = annual rate (as a decimal)
- t = time (in years)

Total amount = $P + I$

Comparing Two Savings Accounts

You have $\$1{,}000$ to deposit. Bank A offers 3% simple interest. Bank B offers 4.5%. You plan to save for 2 years. Which bank earns more?

Bank A: $I = 1{,}000 \times 0.03 \times 2 = \$60$. Total $= \$1{,}060$.

Bank B: $I = 1{,}000 \times 0.045 \times 2 = \$90$. Total $= \$1{,}090$.

Answer: Bank B earns $\$30$ more. A higher rate means more interest.

Savings vs. Borrowing

Interest works in two directions. When you **save**, the bank pays **you** interest — your money grows. When you **borrow**, you pay the bank interest — you owe more than you borrowed. Choosing a higher savings rate or a lower loan rate can save you hundreds of dollars.

> *Always convert the percent rate to a decimal first! $4\% = 0.04$, not 4. Forgetting this gives an answer that is 100 times too large!*

Simple Interest

1. You deposit $\$800$ at 5% for 2 years. How much interest do you earn?
2. You borrow $\$1{,}200$ at 6% for 4 years. How much interest do you owe?
3. Account A: $\$500$ at 3% for 3 years. Account B: $\$500$ at 2% for 5 years. Which earns more interest?
4. A loan of $\$2{,}000$ charges $\$240$ interest over 3 years. What is the rate?
5. You want to earn $\$150$ in interest on $\$1{,}500$ at 2.5%. How many years?

2.7 Percent Error: How Close Are Your Estimates?

Learning Goals

- Calculate percent error using the formula
- Apply percent error to measurement and estimation problems

Percent Error

Percent error measures how far off an estimate or measurement is from the actual value.

$$\text{percent error} = \frac{|\text{estimated} - \text{actual}|}{\text{actual}} \times 100$$

The absolute value $|\,|$ means the answer is always positive — it doesn't matter if you guessed too high or too low.

Finding Percent Error

You estimated a room is 12 feet long. The actual length is 14 feet.

$\text{percent error} = \frac{|12 - 14|}{14} \times 100 = \frac{2}{14} \times 100 \approx 14.3\%$

Answer: The percent error is about 14.3%**.**

Why Percent Error Matters

Scientists always report percent error in experiments. A chemist who predicts a reaction will produce 50 g but gets 47 g has a percent error of 6%. The smaller the percent error, the better the estimate.

Percent Error

1. You guessed 30 jelly beans in a jar. The actual count is 25. Find the percent error.
2. A student estimated a book weighs 2 pounds. It actually weighs 2.5 pounds. Find the percent error.
3. A recipe calls for 3 cups of flour. You used 3.2 cups. What is your percent error?
4. A builder estimated a project would cost $\$5{,}000$. The actual cost was $\$4{,}600$. Find the percent error.
5. If your estimate is exactly correct, the percent error is 0%. True ◯ False ◯

2.8 Personal Financial Literacy

Learning Goals

- Compare financial institutions and payment methods
- Understand credit, debit, and how interest affects decisions

Money Management Basics

- **Bank** — holds your money, offers savings and checking accounts
- **Credit union** — similar to a bank, owned by its members (often lower fees)
- **Debit card** — spends money you already have in your account
- **Credit card** — borrows money you must pay back, often with **interest**
- **Interest rate** — the percent a lender charges (or a bank pays you) on money

Comparing Payment Methods

You buy a $\$200$ game console.

Debit card: You pay $\$200$ from your account. Total cost: $\$200$.

Credit card at 18% annual rate, paid after 1 year:

Interest $= 200 \times 0.18 \times 1 = \$36$. Total cost: $\$236$.

Answer: Credit costs $\$36$ more if you wait a year to pay.

TIP
Pay credit card bills on time every month to avoid extra interest charges!

Financial Literacy

1. You charge $150 on a credit card at 15% annual interest. What is the interest after 1 year?

2. Bank A pays 2% interest on savings. Bank B pays 3.5%. You deposit $1,000 for 1 year. How much more does Bank B earn?

3. A debit card lets you spend more than you have in your account. **True** ○ **False** ○

4. Name one advantage and one disadvantage of using a credit card.

5. A checking account charges a $5 monthly fee. A credit union charges $2/month. How much do you save per year at the credit union?

2.9 Financial Literacy — Budgeting, Saving, and Investing

Learning Goals

- Create and analyze a simple budget
- Compare saving and investing options

Budgeting Basics

A **budget** is a plan for your money.

Income − Expenses = Savings

- **Fixed expenses** stay the same each month (rent, phone plan).
- **Variable expenses** change (food, entertainment).
- **Investing** means putting money into something (stocks, bonds) hoping it grows over time. It has **risk** — you could lose money too.

Making a Monthly Budget

Monthly income: $\$1{,}200$. Fixed expenses: $\$700$. Variable expenses: $\$350$.

Savings $= 1{,}200 - 700 - 350 = \$150$

Savings rate: $\frac{150}{1{,}200} = 0.125 = 12.5\%$

Answer: $\$150$ **saved, which is** 12.5% **of income.**

> *Experts suggest saving at least 10% of your income. Even small amounts add up!*

Budgeting and Saving

1. Income: \$2,000/month. Fixed: \$1,100. Variable: \$600. How much is left to save?
2. You save \$50/month at 3% simple interest for 1 year. How much interest do you earn on the total saved?
3. You want to save \$1,200 in 8 months. How much per month?
4. Your food budget is \$400/month. You spend \$425 one month. By what percent did you go over?
5. A savings account earns 2%/year. An investment averages 7%/year but could lose money. Name one reason to choose each.

2.10 Compound Interest Introduction

Learning Goals

- Understand the difference between simple and compound interest
- Calculate compound interest for short periods

Simple vs. Compound Interest

Simple interest is calculated on the **original principal only**.

Compound interest is calculated on the principal **plus** any interest already earned. Your interest earns interest!

$$A = P(1+r)^t$$

- A = total amount after t years
- P = principal (starting amount)
- r = annual interest rate (as a decimal)
- t = number of years

Comparing Simple and Compound Interest

Deposit $\$500$ at 10% for 3 years.

Simple: $I = 500 \times 0.10 \times 3 = \$150$. Total $= \$650$.

Compound (yearly): Year 1: $500 \times 1.10 = \$550$ Year 2: $550 \times 1.10 = \$605$ Year 3: $605 \times 1.10 = \$665.50$

Answer: Compound earns $\$15.50$ more than simple.

> *Compound interest is like a snowball — it starts small but grows faster and faster!*

Compound Interest

1. You deposit $\$1{,}000$ at 5% compounded yearly. Find the total after 2 years.
2. $\$200$ at 10% simple interest for 2 years vs. compound. Find both totals.
3. Use $A = P(1+r)^t$ to find the value of $\$800$ at 4% for 3 years.
4. Why does compound interest grow faster than simple interest?
5. A $\$600$ loan at 8% compounds yearly for 2 years. How much is owed?

CHAPTER

3

Operations with Rational Numbers

What's Inside

3.1 Integers and Their Opposites

Learning Goals

- Identify integers and their opposites on a number line
- Find absolute values and understand what they measure

Integers and Opposites

Integers are whole numbers and their negatives: $\ldots, -3, -2, -1, 0, 1, 2, 3, \ldots$ Every integer has an **opposite** — the number that is the same distance from 0 on the other side.

- The opposite of 5 is -5. The opposite of -3 is 3.
- A number plus its opposite always equals 0: $5 + (-5) = 0$.
- The **absolute value** $|n|$ is the distance from 0. It is always positive or zero.

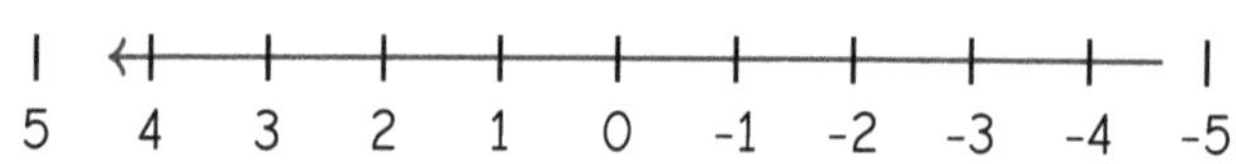

Real-World Opposites

A diver descends 40 feet below sea level, then rises 40 feet.

Descent: -40 ft. Rise: $+40$ ft.

$-40 + 40 = 0$ ⊠ back at sea level.

Answer: Opposite actions cancel to 0.

> *Think of opposites as "undo" buttons. Earning \$20 and spending \$20 puts you right back where you started!*

Integers and Their Opposites

1. What is the opposite of -8?
2. Find $|-12|$ and $|7|$.
3. A football team gains 6 yards, then loses 6 yards. Write this with integers and find the result.
4. The absolute value of a number can be negative. **True** ◯ **False** ◯
5. Order from least to greatest: $-4,\ 2,\ -7,\ 0,\ 5.$

3.2 Adding Integers

Learning Goals

- Add integers using number line reasoning
- Understand that a number plus its opposite equals zero

Rules for Adding Integers

- **Same signs:** Add the absolute values. Keep the sign.

  $5 + 3 = 8$ $(-5) + (-3) = -8$
- **Different signs:** Subtract the smaller absolute value from the larger. Keep the sign of the larger.

  $7 + (-4) = 3$ $(-7) + 4 = -3$
- **Additive inverses:** A number plus its opposite is always 0.

  $9 + (-9) = 0$

Adding on a Number Line

Find $(-3) + 5$.

Start at -3. Adding 5 means move 5 units **right**.

$-3 \to -2 \to -1 \to 0 \to 1 \to 2$

Answer: $(-3) + 5 = 2$

TIP

Think of positive numbers as steps right and negative numbers as steps left. The number line never lies!

Adding Integers

1. $(-8)+(-5)$
2. $(-12)+7$
3. $15+(-15)$
4. The temperature is -6°C in the morning. By noon it rises $14°$. What is the noon temperature?
5. $(-9)+(-4)+6$

★ 3.3 Subtracting Integers ★

Learning Goals

- Rewrite subtraction as adding the opposite
- Find the distance between two integers on a number line

Subtraction = Adding the Opposite

To subtract an integer, **add its opposite**:

$$p - q = p + (-q)$$

- $8 - 3 = 8 + (-3) = 5$
- $4 - 9 = 4 + (-9) = -5$
- $(-2) - 5 = (-2) + (-5) = -7$
- $(-6) - (-4) = (-6) + 4 = -2$

The **distance** between two numbers is $|a - b|$, always positive.

Keep–Change–Flip

Find $(-3) - (-8)$.

Keep the first number: -3.

Change subtraction to addition.

Flip the sign of the second number: $-8 \to +8$.

$(-3) + 8 = 5$

Answer: $(-3) \quad - \quad (-8) \quad = \quad 5$

Watch the Double Negative

~~$(-5) - (-3) = -5 - 3 = -8$~~ $\longrightarrow$ ________________

Subtracting a negative flips it to positive: $(-5) - (-3) = (-5) + 3 = -2$.

Subtracting Integers

1. $10 - 16$
2. $(-7) - (-12)$
3. The temperature dropped from $5°C$ to $-8°C$. What was the change?
4. Find the distance between -9 and 4 on a number line.
5. $(-3) - 5 - (-10)$

★ 3.4 Adding and Subtracting Rational Numbers ★

Learning Goals

- Add and subtract positive and negative fractions and decimals
- Apply integer rules to all rational numbers

Same Rules, New Numbers

The same sign rules from integers work for **all rational numbers** — fractions and decimals too.

- **Same signs:** Add absolute values, keep the sign.
- **Different signs:** Subtract absolute values, keep the sign of the larger.
- For fractions, find a **common denominator** first, then apply the rules.

Adding Signed Fractions

Find $-\frac{2}{3} + \frac{1}{4}$.

Common denominator: 12.

$-\frac{8}{12} + \frac{3}{12}$

Different signs ⊠ subtract: $8 - 3 = 5$. Larger absolute value is negative.

Answer: $-\frac{5}{12}$

“Convert to a common denominator first, then treat the numerators like integers. The sign rules are exactly the same!”

Adding and Subtracting Rational Numbers

1. $-3.5 + 1.8$
2. $-\frac{1}{2} - \frac{3}{4}$
3. $4.2 + (-6.7)$
4. $\frac{5}{6} - \left(-\frac{1}{3}\right)$
5. A diver is at -12.5 m. She goes up 4.8 m, then down 3.2 m. What is her position?

3.5 Multiplying Integers and Rational Numbers

Learning Goals

- Apply the sign rules for multiplication
- Multiply signed fractions and decimals

Sign Rules for Multiplication

Signs	Result	Example
$(+) \times (+)$	Positive	$3 \times 4 = 12$
$(-) \times (-)$	Positive	$(-3)(-4) = 12$
$(+) \times (-)$	Negative	$3 \times (-4) = -12$
$(-) \times (+)$	Negative	$(-3) \times 4 = -12$

Same signs ⊠ positive. Different signs ⊠ negative.

These rules apply to all rational numbers: integers, fractions, and decimals.

Multiplying Signed Fractions

Find $\left(-\frac{2}{3}\right) \times \frac{3}{5}$.

Multiply numerators: $2 \times 3 = 6$. Multiply denominators: $3 \times 5 = 15$.

Different signs ⊠ negative: $-\frac{6}{15} = -\frac{2}{5}$

Answer: $-\frac{2}{5}$

Count the negative signs. An even number of negatives gives a positive product. An odd number gives a negative product.

Multiplying Integers and Rational Numbers

1. $(-6) \times (-9)$
2. $(-4) \times 7$
3. $\left(-\frac{3}{4}\right) \times \left(-\frac{2}{5}\right)$
4. $(-1.5) \times 0.4$
5. $(-2) \times (-3) \times (-5)$

★ 3.6 Dividing Integers and Rational Numbers ★

Learning Goals

- Apply the sign rules for division
- Divide signed fractions and decimals

Sign Rules for Division

Division follows the **same sign rules** as multiplication:

- **Same signs ⊠ positive:** $(-12) \div (-3) = 4$
- **Different signs ⊠ negative:** $12 \div (-3) = -4$

A negative sign can go in front of the fraction, on top, or on bottom — they are all equal:

$$-\frac{p}{q} = \frac{-p}{q} = \frac{p}{-q}$$

You can never divide by zero. $5 \div 0$ is undefined.

Dividing Signed Fractions

Find $-\frac{3}{4} \div \frac{2}{3}$.

Flip the second fraction and multiply: $-\frac{3}{4} \times \frac{3}{2} = -\frac{9}{8}$

Different signs ⊠ negative.

Answer: $-\frac{9}{8}$ **or** $-1\frac{1}{8}$

TIP
Dividing by a fraction is the same as multiplying by its reciprocal. Then use the sign rules you already know!

Dividing Integers and Rational Numbers

1. $(-48) \div (-6)$
2. $35 \div (-7)$
3. $\frac{5}{6} \div \left(-\frac{1}{3}\right)$
4. $(-4.8) \div 1.2$
5. A submarine descends 240 m in 8 minutes at a constant rate. Write the rate as a signed number.

3.7 Converting Rational Numbers to Decimals

Learning Goals

- Convert fractions to decimals using long division
- Recognize terminating and repeating decimals

Terminating vs. Repeating Decimals

Every rational number becomes a decimal that either **terminates** (ends) or **repeats** (a pattern goes on forever).

- **Terminating:** $\frac{3}{8} = 0.375$ — the division comes out even.
- **Repeating:** $\frac{1}{3} = 0.333\ldots = 0.\overline{3}$ — the digit 3 repeats forever.

Use a **bar** over the repeating digits: $\frac{2}{11} = 0.\overline{18}$ means $0.181818\ldots$

Long Division to Find the Decimal

Convert $\frac{5}{6}$ to a decimal.

$5 \div 6 = 0.8333\ldots$

The digit 3 starts repeating, so $\frac{5}{6} = 0.8\overline{3}$.

Answer: $0.8\overline{3}$

> *If the only prime factors of the denominator are 2 and 5, the decimal terminates. Any other prime factor means it repeats!*

Converting Rational Numbers to Decimals

1. Convert $\frac{7}{8}$ to a decimal.
2. Convert $\frac{4}{9}$ to a decimal.
3. Convert $\frac{5}{11}$ to a decimal.
4. $\frac{3}{5}$ is a repeating decimal. True ○ False ○
5. Convert $-\frac{7}{12}$ to a decimal.

★ 3.8 Solving Real-World Problems with Rational Numbers ★

Learning Goals

- Solve multi-step problems using all four operations with rational numbers
- Choose the right operation and check that answers make sense

Putting It All Together

Real-world problems often mix addition, subtraction, multiplication, and division — sometimes with fractions **and** decimals in the same problem.

- **Read carefully.** Decide which operation each part of the problem needs.
- **Watch the signs.** Gains, deposits, and increases are positive. Losses, withdrawals, and decreases are negative.
- **Check your answer.** Does the sign make sense? Is the size reasonable?

Multi-Step Bank Problem

You have $\$125.50$ in your account. You withdraw $\$40.75$, then deposit $\$18.20$, then pay a $\$3.50$ fee. What is your balance?

$125.50 - 40.75 + 18.20 - 3.50$

$= 84.75 + 18.20 - 3.50 = 102.95 - 3.50 = 99.45$

Answer: Balance: $\$99.45$

Temperature and Elevation

Scientists use negative numbers every day. A weather station at -50 m elevation records -12.5°C at midnight. By noon the temperature rises $\frac{3}{4}$ of the way to 0°C. Noon temperature: $-12.5 + \frac{3}{4}(12.5) = -12.5 + 9.375 = -3.125$°C.

Solving Real-World Problems

1. A stock opens at $\$42.30$. It goes up $\$1.75$, down $\$3.20$, and up $\$0.85$. What is the closing price?
2. A recipe needs $2\frac{1}{4}$ cups of liquid. You use $\frac{2}{3}$ cup of milk and the rest is water. How much water?
3. A football team gains 3 yards, loses 7 yards, gains 12 yards, and loses 2 yards. What is the net yardage?
4. You split a $\$48.60$ bill equally among 4 friends. Each friend also pays a $\$2.50$ tip. How much does each person pay total?
5. Evaluate: $-\frac{1}{2} \times 8 + \frac{3}{4} \div \left(-\frac{1}{2}\right)$

CHAPTER

4

Algebraic Expressions

What's Inside

4.1 Writing and Evaluating Expressions

Learning Goals

- Translate word phrases into algebraic expressions
- Evaluate expressions by substituting values for variables

From Words to Algebra

An **algebraic expression** uses numbers, variables, and operations.

Words	Expression
5 more than a number	$n+5$
3 times a number minus 7	$3n-7$
half of a number plus 4	$\frac{n}{2}+4$

To **evaluate**, replace each variable with a number and compute.

Evaluating with Rational Numbers

Evaluate $2x-\frac{3}{4}$ when $x=-1.5$.

Substitute: $2(-1.5)-\frac{3}{4}=-3-0.75=-3.75$

Answer: -3.75

> *Always use parentheses when you substitute a negative number. Writing* $2(-1.5)$ *keeps you from losing the negative sign!*

Writing and Evaluating Expressions

1. Write an expression: "8 less than 3 times a number n."
2. Evaluate $4a + 7$ when $a = -2$.
3. Evaluate $\frac{x}{3} - 5$ when $x = 12$.
4. A phone plan charges \$0.10 per text plus a \$15 monthly fee. Write an expression for the total cost if you send t texts.
5. Using the expression above, find the cost for 85 texts.

★ 4.2 Combining Like Terms ★

Learning Goals

- Identify like terms in an expression
- Simplify expressions by combining like terms

Like Terms

Like terms have the same variable raised to the same power.

- $3x$ and $7x$ are like terms ⊠ combine to $10x$
- $5y$ and $5y^2$ are **not** like terms (different powers)
- Constants like 4 and -9 are always like terms ⊠ combine to -5

The number in front of a variable is the **coefficient**. In $7x$, the coefficient is 7.

Simplifying Step by Step

Simplify $4x + 3 - 2x + 8$.

Group like terms: $(4x - 2x) + (3 + 8)$

Combine: $2x + 11$

Answer: $2x + 11$

Can't Combine Unlike Terms

~~$3x + 5 = 8x$~~ $\longrightarrow$ ______________

$3x$ is a variable term and 5 is a constant. They are not like terms. Correct: $3x + 5$ is already simplified.

Combining Like Terms

1. Simplify $6a + 2a - 3$.
2. Simplify $5x - 9 + 3x + 4$.
3. Simplify $-2y + 7 + 6y - 10$.
4. Simplify $\frac{1}{2}n + \frac{3}{4}n - 2$.
5. $4x + 4y$ can be simplified to $8xy$. True ○ False ○

4.3 Expanding with the Distributive Property

Learning Goals

- Use the distributive property to expand expressions
- Expand with negative and rational coefficients

The Distributive Property

Multiply the number outside the parentheses by **every term** inside:

$$a(b+c) = ab + ac$$

- $3(2x+5) = 6x + 15$
- $-2(4x-3) = -8x + 6$ (watch the signs!)

Expanding with a Negative

Expand $-4(3x-7)$.

Multiply -4 by each term:

$-4 \times 3x = -12x$

$-4 \times (-7) = +28$

Result: $-12x + 28$

> *A negative times a negative gives a positive. So $-4(3x-7)$ gives $-12x+28$, not $-12x-28$!*

Expanding with the Distributive Property

1. Expand $5(2x+3)$.
2. Expand $-3(4a-2)$.
3. Expand $\frac{1}{2}(6x-10)$.
4. Expand and simplify $2(3x+1)+4x$.
5. Expand and simplify $-2(x-5)+3(2x+1)$.

4.4 Factoring Expressions

Learning Goals

- Factor linear expressions by finding the greatest common factor
- Connect factoring to the distributive property in reverse

Factoring = Distributive Property in Reverse

Factoring means rewriting an expression as a product. Find the **greatest common factor (GCF)** of all terms, then divide each term by it:

$$6x + 15 = 3(2x + 5)$$

- GCF of $6x$ and 15 is 3.
- Divide: $6x \div 3 = 2x$ and $15 \div 3 = 5$.
- Write: $3(2x + 5)$.

Check by expanding: $3(2x + 5) = 6x + 15$ ✓

Factoring with a Negative

Factor $-8a + 12$.

GCF of 8 and 12 is 4. Factor out -4:

$-8a \div (-4) = 2a$ $\quad$ $12 \div (-4) = -3$

$-4(2a - 3)$

Check: $-4(2a - 3) = -8a + 12$ ✓

Answer: $-4(2a - 3)$

TIP

Always check your factoring by expanding back out. If you get the original expression, you factored correctly!

Factoring Expressions

1. Factor $10x + 25$.
2. Factor $12y - 18$.
3. Factor $14a + 21b$.
4. Factor $-9x - 6$.
5. $4x + 9$ can be factored. True ○ False ○

4.5 Adding and Subtracting Linear Expressions

Learning Goals

- Add linear expressions by combining like terms
- Subtract linear expressions by distributing the negative sign

Adding and Subtracting Expressions

Adding: Remove parentheses and combine like terms.

$$(3x+5)+(2x-4)=5x+1$$

Subtracting: Distribute the negative to **every term** in the second expression, then combine.

$$(3x+5)-(2x-4)=3x+5-2x+4=x+9$$

Subtracting flips every sign in the second expression.

Subtracting Expressions

Simplify $(7a-3)-(4a+5)$.

Distribute the negative: $7a-3-4a-5$

Combine like terms: $(7a-4a)+(-3-5)=3a-8$

Answer: $3a - 8$

Don't Forget the Second Term

~~$(5x+2)-(3x-1)=5x+2-3x-1=2x+1$~~ $\longrightarrow$ ____________

The negative must flip **both** signs: $-3x$ and $+1$. Correct: $5x+2-3x+1=2x+3$.

Adding and Subtracting Linear Expressions

1. $(4x+6)+(3x-2)$
2. $(8n-5)-(3n+7)$
3. $(2y+9)-(2y-1)$
4. $(-x+4)+(6x-8)$
5. Perimeter of a triangle with sides $2x+1$, $3x-4$, and $x+5$.

4.6 Rewriting Expressions to Solve Problems

Learning Goals

- Rewrite expressions in different forms to reveal useful information
- Connect equivalent expressions to real-world meaning

Different Forms, Same Value

The same situation can be written in different ways, and each form tells you something different.

Form	What it tells you
$a + 0.05a$	Start with a, add 5% of a
$1.05a$	Total is 105% of a (simpler to compute)

Both are equivalent: $a + 0.05a = 1a + 0.05a = 1.05a$. Rewriting helps you compute faster or see the problem differently.

Seeing the Big Picture

A gym charges \$30 per month. A coupon gives 20% off.

Form 1: $30 - 0.20(30) = 30 - 6 = 24$ (compute the discount, then subtract)

Form 2: $0.80(30) = 24$ (multiply by what you keep: 80%)

Both give \$24, but Form 2 is one step instead of two.

Answer: Rewriting $p - 0.20p$ as $0.80p$ is faster.

Is It Really a Better Deal?

A store says "Buy 2, get 1 free!" That sounds like 33% off. But if each shirt is $\$s$, you pay $2s$ for 3 shirts. Price per shirt: $\frac{2s}{3} = \frac{2}{3}s \approx 0.67s$. That is about 33% off each shirt. Rewriting the expression confirmed it!

Rewriting Expressions

1. Rewrite $x + 0.08x$ as a single term. What does it represent?
2. A price p is discounted 15%. Write two equivalent expressions for the sale price.
3. Rewrite $3(x + 4) - 2x$ in simplest form.
4. A worker earns $\$h$ per hour plus $\$50$ bonus, working 40 hours a week. Write an expression for weekly pay and simplify.
5. Show that "increase by 25% then decrease by 20%" gives back the original price.

CHAPTER

5

Equations and Inequalities

What's Inside

5.1 Writing Two-Step Equations

Learning Goals

- Translate real-world problems into equations of the form $px + q = r$
- Identify the variable, rate, and starting value in a situation

From Words to Equations

A **two-step equation** has a variable that is multiplied **and** added to (or subtracted from):

$$px + q = r$$

Situation	Equation
Earn \$8/hr plus \$20 bonus, total \$100	$8h + 20 = 100$
3 pizzas plus \$5 delivery = \$32	$3p + 5 = 32$
Spend \$4/day from \$50, left with \$18	$50 - 4d = 18$

Setting Up the Equation

A gym charges \$25 to join plus \$10 per month. You have spent \$85 total. How many months have you been a member?

Let $m =$ months. Total: $10m + 25 = 85$.

Answer: $10m + 25 = 85$

> “Look for the rate (per something) — that goes with the variable. Look for the fixed amount — that is the constant.”

Writing Two-Step Equations

1. You buy n notebooks at $\$3$ each and a $\$7$ binder. The total is $\$22$. Write an equation.
2. A taxi charges $\$2.50$ per mile plus a $\$3$ base fare. The ride costs $\$18$. Write an equation for the miles m.
3. You have $\$60$. You spend $\$8$ per week. After how many weeks will you have $\$12$ left? Write an equation.
4. A phone plan charges $\$0.05$ per text plus $\$15$ monthly. The bill is $\$21.50$. Write an equation for texts t.
5. Write an equation: “Five times a number minus 9 equals 31.”

5.2 Solving Two-Step Equations

Learning Goals

- Solve equations of the form $px + q = r$ by undoing operations
- Check answers by substituting back into the original equation

Undo in Reverse Order

To solve a two-step equation, undo the operations **backward**:

- **Step 1:** Undo addition or subtraction (move the constant).
- **Step 2:** Undo multiplication or division (isolate the variable).

$$3x + 7 = 22 \xrightarrow{-7} 3x = 15 \xrightarrow{\div 3} x = 5$$

Always check: $3(5) + 7 = 15 + 7 = 22$ ✓

Solving Step by Step

Solve $\dfrac{x}{4} - 3 = 5$.

Add 3 to both sides: $\dfrac{x}{4} = 8$

Multiply both sides by 4: $x = 32$

Check: $\frac{32}{4} - 3 = 8 - 3 = 5$ ✓

Answer: $x = 32$

TIP
Whatever you do to one side, do the exact same thing to the other side. That keeps the equation balanced!

Solving Two-Step Equations

1. Solve $2x + 9 = 25$.
2. Solve $5n - 12 = 33$.
3. Solve $\frac{y}{3} + 7 = 15$.
4. Solve $-4x + 10 = -6$.
5. A gym charges $\$10$ per month plus $\$25$ to join. You spent $\$85$. How many months?

5.3 Solving Equations with the Distributive Property

Learning Goals

- Solve equations of the form $p(x+q)=r$
- Choose between distributing first or dividing first

Two Approaches

For equations like $3(x+4)=27$, you can solve two ways:

- **Distribute first:** $3x+12=27$ ⊠ solve as a two-step equation.
- **Divide first:** $x+4=9$ ⊠ solve in one step.

Both give the same answer. Pick whichever feels easier.

Comparing Methods

Solve $4(x-2)=20$.

Method 1 — Distribute:

$4x-8=20$

$4x=28 \rightarrow x=7$

Method 2 — Divide by 4:

$x-2=5$

$x=7$ ✓

> *If the number outside the parentheses divides evenly into the other side, dividing first is faster!*

Solving with the Distributive Property

1. Solve $2(x+5)=18$.
2. Solve $5(n-3)=-10$.
3. Solve $-3(y+4)=15$.
4. Solve $6(2x-1)=42$.
5. Each side of a square is $(x+3)$ cm. The perimeter is 52 cm. Find x.

5.4 Solving Multi-Step Problems with Rational Numbers

Learning Goals

- Solve multi-step equations with fractions and decimals
- Use estimation to check that answers are reasonable

Handling Fractions and Decimals

Some equations have fraction or decimal coefficients. Two strategies:

- **Multiply to clear fractions:** Multiply every term by the LCD.
  $\frac{x}{3} + \frac{1}{2} = 5$ ⊠ multiply by 6: $2x + 3 = 30$
- **Work with decimals directly:** Use standard operations.
  $0.25x + 1.5 = 4$ ⊠ subtract 1.5: $0.25x = 2.5$ ⊠ $x = 10$

Clearing Fractions

Solve $\dfrac{2x}{5} - 3 = 7$.

Add 3: $\dfrac{2x}{5} = 10$

Multiply by 5: $2x = 50$

Divide by 2: $x = 25$

Check: $\frac{2(25)}{5} - 3 = 10 - 3 = 7$ ✓

Answer: $x = 25$

TIP

Before solving, estimate the answer. If the equation says $0.5x + 3 = 10$, then x should be around 14. If you get 140, you probably made a decimal mistake!

Multi-Step Problems with Rational Numbers

1. Solve $0.3x + 2.1 = 5.1$.
2. Solve $\frac{x}{4} + \frac{3}{4} = 5$.
3. Solve $-1.5y + 4 = -8$.
4. Solve $\frac{3n}{2} - 5 = 10$.
5. A store marks down shirts by $\frac{1}{3}$ of the price, then takes off another \$4. The final price is \$12. What was the original price?

5.5 Writing and Solving Inequalities

Learning Goals

- Write inequalities from word problems
- Solve two-step inequalities, including when to flip the sign

Inequalities

An **inequality** compares two expressions using $<$, $>$, $\leq$, or $\geq$.

Solve just like equations, with **one key rule**:

When you multiply or divide by a negative number, flip the inequality sign.

$$-2x > 6 \xrightarrow{\div(-2)} x < -3$$

Words	Symbol
at least, no less than	$\geq$
at most, no more than	$\leq$
more than	$>$
fewer than, less than	$<$

Solving a Two-Step Inequality

Solve $3x - 7 \leq 14$.

Add 7: $3x \leq 21$

Divide by 3: $x \leq 7$

Answer: $x \leq 7$

Forgetting to Flip

~~$-5x > 20$ ⊠ $x > -4$~~ $\longrightarrow$ ____________

When dividing by a negative, flip the sign. Correct: $-5x > 20$ ⊠ $x < -4$.

Writing and Solving Inequalities

1. Solve $2x + 5 > 17$.
2. Solve $-3n + 9 \leq 0$.
3. You have \$50 and spend \$6 per day. After how many days will you have less than \$14?
4. Solve $\frac{x}{4} - 2 \geq 3$.
5. A student needs at least 80 points on a test. She earns 5 points per question and starts with 15 bonus points. How many questions must she answer correctly?

5.6 Graphing Inequalities on a Number Line

Learning Goals

- Graph inequality solutions using open and closed circles
- Interpret graphs in real-world contexts

Graphing Inequality Solutions

Draw the solution on a number line:

- **Open circle** ○: the endpoint is **not** included ($<$ or $>$).
- **Closed circle** ●: the endpoint **is** included ($\leq$ or $\geq$).
- **Shade** the direction of all solutions.

$x > 3$ open circle at 3, shade right

$x \leq -1$ closed circle at -1, shade left

Solve and Graph

Solve $2x - 1 < 5$ and graph the solution.

Add 1: $2x < 6$. Divide by 2: $x < 3$.

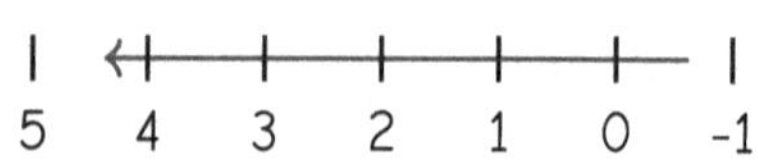

Open circle at 3, shade everything to the left.

Answer: $x < 3$

> *Think of the circle as a gate. Open = "you can't come in." Closed = "you're included!"*

Graphing Solutions to Inequalities

1. Solve and describe the graph: $x + 4 \geq 7$.
2. Solve and describe the graph: $3n - 6 > 0$.
3. Solve and describe the graph: $-2x \leq 8$.
4. The graph of $x < 5$ uses a closed circle at 5. True ◯ False ◯
5. A parking lot charges \$3 per hour. You have \$20. Write and solve an inequality for how many hours h you can park. Describe the graph.

CHAPTER

6

Scale Drawings, Geometric Figures, and Angle Relationships

What's Inside

6.1 Understanding and Using Scale Drawings

Learning Goals

- Use scale factors to find actual lengths from a scale drawing
- Understand how scale affects area

Scale Drawings

A **scale drawing** is a proportional copy of a real object — every length is multiplied by the same **scale factor**.

$$\text{actual length} = \text{drawing length} \times \text{scale factor}$$

If the scale is "1 cm $= 5$ m," then the scale factor is 5. A 3 cm wall on the drawing is $3 \times 5 = 15$ m in real life.

Area scales differently: if lengths scale by k, areas scale by k^2.

Using a Map Scale

A map uses the scale 1 cm $= 20$ km. Two cities are 4.5 cm apart on the map. What is the actual distance?

$4.5 \times 20 = 90$ km

Answer: The actual distance is 90 km.

> *“Scale drawings keep all shapes proportional. Angles stay the same — only lengths change!”*

Scale Drawings

1. A blueprint uses the scale 1 in $= 8$ ft. A room is 2.5 in wide on the blueprint. What is the actual width?

2. On a map, 3 cm $= 45$ km. What is the scale factor?

3. A model car is 6 inches long. The scale is $1 : 24$. How long is the real car?

4. A rectangle on a blueprint is 2 cm by 3 cm. The scale is 1 cm $= 4$ m. Find the actual area.

5. If a scale factor doubles all lengths, the area also doubles. **True** ○ **False** ○

6.2 Reproducing Scale Drawings at a Different Scale

Learning Goals

- Convert a scale drawing to a new scale
- Calculate the new scale factor from two given scales

Changing the Scale

To redraw at a new scale, find how the two scales relate:

$$\text{new drawing length} = \text{old drawing length} \times \frac{\text{new scale factor}}{\text{old scale factor}}$$

Example: Old scale: 1 cm $= 10$ m. New scale: 1 cm $= 5$ m.

Ratio: $\frac{10}{5} = 2$. Every old measurement is multiplied by 2 on the new drawing.

A 3 cm line becomes $3 \times 2 = 6$ cm.

Rescaling a Floor Plan

A floor plan uses 1 cm $= 8$ ft. You want to redraw it at 1 cm $= 4$ ft. A wall is 5 cm on the original. How long is it on the new drawing?

Scale ratio: $\frac{8}{4} = 2$. New length: $5 \times 2 = 10$ cm.

Answer: 10 **cm on the new drawing.**

TIP

Going to a larger scale (fewer real units per cm) makes the drawing bigger. Going to a smaller scale makes it smaller.

Reproducing Scale Drawings

1. A map uses 1 cm $= 50$ km. You redraw it at 1 cm $= 25$ km. A 4 cm road becomes how long?
2. A model uses scale $1 : 100$. You need scale $1 : 50$. A 3 cm wall becomes how long?
3. A drawing uses 1 cm $= 2$ m. Redraw at 1 cm $= 6$ m. A 9 cm room becomes how long?
4. A rectangle is 4 cm by 6 cm on the original map (1 cm $= 10$ m). What is its area on a new map at 1 cm $= 5$ m?
5. Changing the scale of a drawing changes the angles in the shapes. True ◯ False ◯

6.3 Drawing Geometric Figures with Given Conditions

Learning Goals

- Draw shapes that meet specific side-length and angle conditions
- Determine when conditions produce one, many, or no shapes

When Can You Draw a Shape?

Given conditions may produce:

- **Exactly one shape** — the conditions fully determine it (e.g., three sides of a triangle with valid lengths).
- **More than one shape** — the conditions allow flexibility (e.g., a quadrilateral with four given sides can have different angles).
- **No shape** — the conditions are impossible (e.g., a triangle with sides 2, 3, 10 — violates the triangle inequality).

Testing Conditions

Can you draw a triangle with sides 5 cm, 7 cm, and 3 cm?

Check the **triangle inequality**: the sum of any two sides must be greater than the third.

- $5 + 7 = 12 > 3$ ✓
- $5 + 3 = 8 > 7$ ✓
- $7 + 3 = 10 > 5$ ✓

Answer: Yes — all three checks pass.

"Think of it like building with sticks. If one stick is longer than the other two combined, they can't connect to form a triangle!"

Drawing Geometric Figures

1. Can you draw a triangle with sides 4 cm, 6 cm, and 11 cm?
2. Can you draw a triangle with sides 5, 5, and 5?
3. A rectangle has a perimeter of 20 cm. How many different rectangles are possible?
4. You know two sides of a triangle are 6 cm and 8 cm, and the angle between them is $90°$. How many triangles can you draw?
5. If you know all three angles of a triangle, there is exactly one triangle you can draw. True ○ False ○

6.4 Constructing Triangles from Three Measurements

Learning Goals

- Determine when three measurements produce a unique triangle, more than one, or none
- Apply the triangle inequality and angle sum rules

Triangle Conditions

Given	Result
Three sides (SSS)	Unique triangle (if inequality holds)
Two sides + included angle (SAS)	Unique triangle
Two angles + included side (ASA)	Unique triangle
Two angles + non-included side (AAS)	Unique triangle
Three angles (AAA)	Many triangles (same shape, different sizes)

Key facts:

- Triangle inequality: each side $<$ sum of the other two.
- Angle sum: the three angles must add to $180°$.

Checking Angle Conditions

Can you draw a triangle with angles $50°$, $60°$, and $80°$?

$50 + 60 + 80 = 190°$. But triangle angles must sum to $180°$.

Answer: No triangle is possible.

TIP

If you know two angles, you can always find the third: $180°$ – angle 1 – angle 2.

Constructing Triangles

1. Can a triangle have angles $35°$, $65°$, and $80°$? If so, is it unique?
2. Sides 7, 10, 15. Can a triangle be formed? Is it unique?
3. Sides 3, 4, and included angle $90°$. Unique?
4. Can a triangle have angles $90°$, $90°$, and $0°$?
5. Two angles of a triangle are $40°$ and $70°$. What is the third angle?

6.5 Cross-Sections of 3D Figures

Learning Goals

- Describe the 2D shape formed by slicing a 3D figure with a plane
- Identify cross-sections of prisms and pyramids

What Is a Cross-Section?

A **cross-section** is the flat shape you see when you slice through a 3D figure with a plane — like cutting a loaf of bread.

- **Right rectangular prism** (box): slices can be rectangles, squares, or triangles, depending on the angle of the cut.
- **Right rectangular pyramid**: slices can be triangles, trapezoids, or rectangles.

The shape depends on **where** and **at what angle** you cut.

Slicing a Rectangular Prism

Imagine slicing a box of cereal:

- **Horizontal cut** (parallel to the base): rectangle
- **Vertical cut** (parallel to one face): rectangle
- **Diagonal cut** (corner to corner): triangle or other polygon

Answer: The cross-section shape depends on the angle of the slice.

> *Every horizontal slice of a prism looks exactly like the base. Cut parallel to the base and you always get the same shape!*

Cross-Sections of 3D Figures

1. You slice a rectangular prism with a cut parallel to its base. What shape is the cross-section?

2. You slice a rectangular pyramid with a horizontal cut parallel to its base, halfway up. What shape do you get?

3. You cut a cube with a diagonal slice from one edge to the opposite edge. What shape could the cross-section be?

4. Every cross-section of a sphere is a circle. **True** ○ **False** ○

5. A cone is sliced with a horizontal cut parallel to its base. What shape is the cross-section?

6.6 Angle Relationships

Learning Goals

- Identify supplementary, complementary, and vertical angle pairs
- Write and solve equations to find unknown angles

Angle Pairs

- **Complementary angles** add to $90°$. $\angle A + \angle B = 90°$
- **Supplementary angles** add to $180°$. $\angle A + \angle B = 180°$
- **Vertical angles** are formed by two intersecting lines. They are always **equal**.
- **Adjacent angles** share a side and a vertex.

Finding an Unknown Angle

Two angles are supplementary. One angle is $3x + 10$ and the other is $2x$. Find both angles.

$3x + 10 + 2x = 180$

$5x + 10 = 180$ ⊠ $5x = 170$ ⊠ $x = 34$

Angles: $3(34) + 10 = 112°$ and $2(34) = 68°$.

Check: $112 + 68 = 180°$ ✓

Answer: $112°$ **and** $68°$

TIP

Vertical angles are always equal. If you spot an X made by two lines, the opposite angles match!

Angle Relationships

1. Two angles are complementary. One is $35°$. Find the other.
2. Two angles are supplementary. One is $128°$. Find the other.
3. Two vertical angles are $4x + 5$ and $6x - 15$. Find x and the angle measure.
4. An angle and its complement are in the ratio $2 : 3$. Find both angles.
5. Two supplementary angles are $(x + 30)°$ and $(2x)°$. Find both.

6.7 Similar Figures and Proportions

Learning Goals

- Identify similar figures and find missing side lengths
- Use scale factors to solve real-world problems

Similar Figures

Two figures are **similar** if they have the same shape but not necessarily the same size.

- Corresponding angles are **equal**.
- Corresponding sides are **proportional** (same scale factor).

$$\frac{\text{side of figure A}}{\text{corresponding side of figure B}} = \text{scale factor}$$

Finding a Missing Side

Triangle $ABC \sim$ Triangle DEF. $AB = 6$, $DE = 9$, $BC = 8$. Find EF.

Scale factor: $\frac{9}{6} = 1.5$

$EF = 8 \times 1.5 = 12$

Answer: $EF = 12$

TIP

Set up a proportion with corresponding sides: $\frac{AB}{DE} = \frac{BC}{EF}$. Cross-multiply to solve!

Similar Figures

1. Rectangle $ABCD \sim$ Rectangle $EFGH$. $AB = 4$, $EF = 10$, $BC = 6$. Find FG.
2. Two similar triangles have sides 5 and 15. What is the scale factor?
3. A tree casts a 12-ft shadow. A 5-ft person casts a 3-ft shadow. How tall is the tree?
4. Triangle $PQR \sim$ Triangle STU. $PQ = 10$, $ST = 4$, $QR = 15$, $PR = 20$. Find TU and SU.
5. A photo is 4 in. by 6 in. It is enlarged so the short side is 10 in. What is the long side?

CHAPTER

7

Circles, Area, Surface Area, and Volume

What's Inside

7.1 Parts of a Circle

Learning Goals

- Identify and describe the center, radius, diameter, and circumference of a circle
- Relate diameter and radius; prepare for circumference and area formulas

Circle Vocabulary

- **Center**: The middle point of the circle
- **Radius**: Distance from center to edge
- **Diameter**: Distance across the circle through the center ($2\times$ radius)
- **Circumference**: The distance around the circle

Labeling Circle Parts

Draw a circle. Mark the center O, a radius OA, and a diameter AB passing through O. Label the circumference as the edge.

Answer: Center O, radius OA, diameter AB, circumference

TIP

The diameter is always twice the radius: $d = 2r$.

Circle Parts

1. What is the radius if the diameter is 10 cm?

2. What is the diameter if the radius is 7 in?

3. Name all parts of a circle shown in a diagram with center O, radius OA, diameter AB, circumference C.

4. If the circumference is 31.4 cm and the diameter is 10 cm, what is π rounded to the nearest tenth?

5. If the radius is 4 m, what is the diameter and circumference (use $\pi \approx 3.14$)?

7.2 Circumference of a Circle

Learning Goals

- Use $C = \pi d$ and $C = 2\pi r$ to find circumference
- Understand the relationship between circumference and diameter

Circumference Formulas

- $C = \pi d$ (diameter)
- $C = 2\pi r$ (radius)

Finding Circumference

Find the circumference of a circle with diameter 12 cm.

$C = \pi d = 3.14 \times 12 = 37.68$ cm

Answer: 37.68 cm

TIP

The ratio C/d is always π for any circle.

Circumference

1. Find the circumference if the radius is 9 m ($\pi \approx 3.14$).
2. Find the circumference if the diameter is 15 in ($\pi \approx 3.14$).
3. A circle has circumference 31.4 cm. What is its diameter?
4. If the radius is 6 ft, what is the circumference?
5. A bike wheel has diameter 0.7 m. How far does it roll in one turn?

7.3 Area of a Circle

Learning Goals

- Use $A = \pi r^2$ to find the area of a circle
- Understand why the formula works

Area Formula

$A = \pi r^2$

Finding Area

Find the area of a circle with radius 5 cm.

$A = \pi r^2 = 3.14 \times 5^2 = 3.14 \times 25 = 78.5$ cm^2

Answer: 78.5 cm^2

TIP
The area formula comes from rearranging the circle into a shape like a parallelogram.

Area of a Circle

1. Find the area if the radius is 8 m ($\pi \approx 3.14$).
2. Find the area if the diameter is 10 in ($\pi \approx 3.14$).
3. A circle has area 50.24 cm^2. What is its radius?
4. If the radius is 3 ft, what is the area?
5. A pizza has diameter 12 in. What is its area?

7.4 Area of Composite Shapes

Learning Goals

- Find the area of figures made of triangles, quadrilaterals, and polygons
- Add and subtract areas to solve real-world problems

Composite Shapes

A composite shape is made by combining simpler shapes.

Finding Area of a Composite Shape

A figure is made of a rectangle 6×4 cm and a semicircle with radius 2 cm attached to one side. Find the total area ($\pi \approx 3.14$).

Rectangle: $6 \times 4 = 24$ cm^2 Semicircle: $A = \frac{1}{2}\pi r^2 = 0.5 \times 3.14 \times 4 = 6.28$ cm^2 Total: $24 + 6.28 = 30.28$ cm^2

Answer: 30.28 cm^2

TIP
Break composite shapes into familiar pieces, find each area, then add or subtract.

Composite Area

1. Find the area of a shape made of a rectangle 8×3 m and a triangle with base 8 m, height 2 m.
2. Find the area of a figure made of a square 5×5 in and a quarter circle with radius 5 in ($\pi \approx 3.14$).
3. A composite shape is a rectangle 10×4 ft with a triangle 10 ft base, 3 ft height attached. Find the total area.
4. Find the area of a figure made of a rectangle 7×2 cm and a semicircle with radius 1 cm ($\pi \approx 3.14$).
5. A composite shape is made of two rectangles 5×3 m and 2×3 m. Find the total area.

7.5 Surface Area of Three-Dimensional Objects

Learning Goals

- Find the surface area of cubes, prisms, and other 3D objects
- Use nets and formulas to calculate total surface area

Surface Area

Surface area is the total area covering the outside of a 3D object.

Surface Area of a Rectangular Prism

Find the surface area of a box $4 \times 3 \times 2$ cm.

$2(4 \times 3) + 2(4 \times 2) + 2(3 \times 2) = 2(12) + 2(8) + 2(6) = 24 + 16 + 12 = 52$ cm^2

Answer: 52 cm^2

TIP: Draw a net to see all faces. Add the area of each face for total surface area.

Surface Area

1. Find the surface area of a cube with side 5 m.
2. Find the surface area of a rectangular prism $7 \times 2 \times 3$ in.
3. A box is $6 \times 4 \times 2$ ft. Find its surface area.
4. Find the surface area of a prism with base 8×3 cm and height 5 cm.
5. A triangular prism has base 6 m, height 4 m, length 10 m. Find surface area.

★ 7.6 Volume of Prisms ★

Learning Goals

- Find the volume of cubes and right prisms using $V = Bh$
- Apply volume formulas to real-world problems

Volume Formula

$V = Bh$ (area of base $\times$ height)

Volume of a Rectangular Prism

Find the volume of a box $5 \times 3 \times 2$ cm.

Base: $5 \times 3 = 15$ cm^2 Height: 2 cm $V = 15 \times 2 = 30$ cm^3

Answer: 30 cm^3

TIP
Volume measures how much space is inside a 3D object.

Volume

1. Find the volume of a cube with side 4 m.
2. Find the volume of a rectangular prism $6 \times 2 \times 5$ in.
3. A box is $8 \times 3 \times 2$ ft. Find its volume.
4. Find the volume of a prism with base 7×2 cm and height 6 cm.
5. A triangular prism has base 5 m, height 3 m, length 12 m. Find volume.

CHAPTER

8

Statistics: Sampling and Comparing Populations

What's Inside

8.1 Populations and Samples

Learning Goals

- Understand populations, samples, and why random sampling matters
- Design simple experiments and plan data collection

Population, Sample, and Experimental Design

- **Population**: The whole group you want to study.
- **Sample**: A smaller group chosen from the population.
- **Random sample**: Every member has an equal chance of being chosen. This avoids **bias**.

Before collecting data, plan your experiment:

1. **Ask a question** — What do you want to find out?
2. **Identify the population** — Who or what are you studying?
3. **Choose a sampling method** — How will you pick your sample?
4. **Collect data** — Gather the information.
5. **Analyze and conclude** — What does the data tell you?

Designing a Survey

A school wants to know the favorite sport of all 600 students. Design a fair experiment.

Question: What sport is most popular among students?

Population: All 600 students.

Method: Use a random number generator to pick 60 student IDs. Survey those 60.

Why random? Surveying only basketball players would bias the results. Random selection gives every student an equal chance.

Answer: A random sample of 60 from 600 avoids bias.

TIP

A sample must be random and representative to give valid results. Bigger samples are usually more reliable, but even a small random sample beats a large biased one.

Populations and Samples

1. A teacher wants to know how much time students spend on homework. She surveys the first 10 students who arrive. Is this a good sample? Explain.
2. Describe the population and sample: A factory tests 50 light bulbs from a batch of $5{,}000$.
3. Design an experiment to find out which school lunch is most popular. List the five steps.
4. Why is random sampling important?
5. A company surveys only its own employees about a new product. What is the problem?

8.2 Making Inferences from Random Samples

Learning Goals

- Use data from random samples to make predictions about a population
- Understand variability in sample estimates

Inference from Samples

Predictions about a population are made using data from a random sample.

Estimating a Population Mean

A random sample of 20 students has an average test score of 82. Predict the average for all 200 students.

Answer: Estimate: 82 is likely close to the population mean, but could vary.

TIP
Multiple random samples may give slightly different results.

Making Inferences

1. A sample of 30 plants has an average height of 15 cm. Predict the average height for all 300 plants.
2. Why do different samples give different estimates?
3. If two samples have means 20 and 22, what does this tell you?
4. How can you improve the reliability of an estimate?
5. What is the risk of using a non-random sample?

8.3 Comparing Two Populations Visually

Learning Goals

- Compare two data distributions by visual overlap
- Measure difference between centers and variability

Visual Comparison

Compare distributions by looking at their graphs and overlap.

Comparing Heights

Class A: mean 150 cm, Class B: mean 155 cm. Both have similar spread. Which is taller?

Answer: Class B is taller on average, but overlap means some students in A are taller than some in B.

TIP

Look at both the center (mean/median) and spread (range, MAD) when comparing.

Comparing Populations

1. Two classes have means 80 and 85. Which is higher?
2. If two groups have overlapping ranges, what does this mean?
3. Why is it important to look at variability?
4. If Group A has mean 70, Group B has mean 75, but Group A has a larger range, what does this mean?
5. What is mean absolute deviation (MAD)?

8.4 Comparing Populations with Measures of Center and Variability

Learning Goals

- Use mean, median, range, and IQR to compare two populations
- Support conclusions with data and reasoning

Measures of Center and Variability

- **Mean**: Add all values, divide by the count.
- **Median**: The middle value when data is ordered.
- **Range**: Highest − lowest. Shows total spread.
- **Interquartile Range (IQR)**: $Q_3 - Q_1$. Spread of the middle 50%.

The **IQR** is often more useful than range because it ignores outliers. Use **multiple** measures — not just one — to compare groups.

Comparing Fish Catch Data

Two fishing crews recorded daily catch (in pounds) over 5 days:

Crew A: $120, 135, 140, 150, 155$ **Crew B:** $90, 130, 145, 160, 200$

	Crew A	Crew B
Mean	140	145
Median	140	145
Range	35	110
IQR	15	30

Crew B catches slightly more on average, but Crew A is **far more consistent**. Crew B's large range and IQR suggest some very high and very low days.

Answer: Crew B averages more, but Crew A is more reliable.

TIP

Range can be thrown off by a single extreme value. IQR focuses on the middle half of the data and gives a better picture of typical spread.

Comparing Populations with Measures

1. Group A: mean 70, median 72, range 20, IQR 8. Group B: mean 75, median 74, range 40, IQR 18. Which group is more consistent?

2. Two students track daily steps for a week. Student X: mean 8,000, IQR 1,500. Student Y: mean 8,200, IQR 4,000. Compare their activity.

3. Why is IQR often better than range for comparing two groups?

4. Data set: $5, 8, 10, 12, 15, 18, 50$. Find the range and IQR. Which better represents the spread?

5. Two classes take a quiz. Class A median: 82, IQR: 6. Class B median: 78, IQR: 14. Which class performed better overall? Explain.

8.5 Stem-and-Leaf Plots

Learning Goals

- Organize data using a stem-and-leaf plot
- Read and interpret stem-and-leaf plots to find measures of center

How Stem-and-Leaf Plots Work

A **stem-and-leaf plot** organizes numbers by splitting each value into a **stem** (all digits except the last) and a **leaf** (the last digit).

Example data: $23, 25, 31, 34, 34, 38, 42$

Stem	Leaf
2	3 5
3	1 4 4 8
4	2

Key: $3 \mid 4$ means 34. Leaves are always written in order.

Finding the Median from a Stem-and-Leaf Plot

Use the plot above. There are 7 values: $23, 25, 31, 34, 34, 38, 42$.

The middle value (4th) is 34.

Answer: Median $= \quad 34$

TIP
Count the total number of leaves to find how many data values there are!

Stem-and-Leaf Plots

1. Make a stem-and-leaf plot for: $15, 18, 22, 25, 27, 31, 33, 38$.

2. From this plot, find the median. Stem 4: $1\ 3\ 5$ Stem 5: $0\ 2\ 7\ 8$ Stem 6: 4

3. What is the range of the data set in Problem 2?

4. How many data values are shown in: Stem 7: $2\ 2\ 5$ Stem 8: $0\ 3\ 6\ 9$ Stem 9: $1\ 4$?

5. In a stem-and-leaf plot, $6 \mid 3$ means 63. True ○ False ○

★ 8.6 Circle Graphs ★

Learning Goals

- Read and interpret circle (pie) graphs
- Relate sectors to fractions, decimals, and percents

Circle Graphs

A **circle graph** (pie chart) shows how a whole is divided into parts. The full circle represents 100% (or $360°$).

- Each **sector** shows one category as a fraction of the whole.
- Sector angle $=$ percent $\times 360°$.
- All sectors must add up to 100% (or $360°$).

Reading a Circle Graph

A survey of 200 students' favorite sport:

Soccer 40%, Basketball 25%, Baseball 20%, Other 15%

How many students chose soccer? $200 \times 0.40 = 80$

What angle for basketball? $0.25 \times 360° = 90°$

Answer: 80 **students chose soccer; basketball sector** $=$ $90°$.

"To check your circle graph, make sure all the percents add to 100%!"

Circle Graphs

1. A circle graph shows that 30% of 500 people prefer cats. How many is that?
2. A sector represents $\frac{1}{4}$ of a data set. What is its angle?
3. Four categories have percents 35%, 25%, 20%, and x%. Find x.
4. In a class of 40 students, 12 walk to school, 20 take the bus, 8 get a ride. What percent walks?
5. A sector has a 72° angle. What percent of the whole does it represent?

CHAPTER

9

Probability and Compound Events

What's Inside

9.1 What Is Probability?

Learning Goals

- Understand probability as a number between 0 and 1
- Interpret probability in terms of likelihood

Probability Basics

- Probability measures how likely an event is to happen
- 0 means impossible, 1 means certain, 0.5 means equally likely or not

Probability Scale

What is the probability of rolling a 7 on a standard die?

Impossible: $P = 0$

Answer: 0

TIP

Probability is always between 0 and 1.

Probability

1. What is the probability of flipping heads on a fair coin?
2. What is the probability of picking a red marble from a bag with 3 red and 7 blue marbles?
3. What does a probability of 1 mean?
4. What does a probability of 0 mean?
5. What does a probability near 0.5 mean?

9.2 Theoretical Probability

Learning Goals

- Calculate theoretical probability using favorable/total outcomes
- Develop uniform probability models

Theoretical Probability

$P = \frac{\text{favorable outcomes}}{\text{total outcomes}}$

Rolling a Die

What is the probability of rolling a 4 on a standard die?

$P = 1/6 \approx 0.167$

Answer: $1/6$ **or** 0.167

TIP
All outcomes must be equally likely for theoretical probability.

Theoretical Probability

1. What is the probability of drawing a heart from a standard deck of 52 cards?
2. What is the probability of rolling an even number on a die?
3. What is the probability of picking a green marble from 5 green and 15 yellow marbles?
4. What is the probability of drawing a 2 or 3 from a deck of cards?
5. What is the probability of rolling a number greater than 4 on a die?

★ 9.3 Experimental Probability ★

Learning Goals

- Approximate probability by collecting data from experiments
- Design and use simulations to estimate probabilities

Experimental Probability and Simulations

Experimental probability uses real data:

$$P(\text{event}) = \frac{\text{number of times event occurs}}{\text{total trials}}$$

A **simulation** models a real situation using simple tools like coins, dice, spinners, or random-number generators. Simulations let you estimate probabilities when real experiments are too slow, expensive, or impractical.

Steps to design a simulation:

1. Identify the event and its possible outcomes.
2. Choose a model (coin, die, random digits) that matches the probabilities.
3. Run many trials and record the results in a frequency table.
4. Calculate the experimental probability and compare to the theoretical value.

Simulating Blood Type Donors

About 30% of donors have type A blood. Use random digits $(0–9)$ to simulate finding the first type A donor. Let digits $0, 1, 2$ represent type A.

Trial	Random digits	Donors until type A
1	7, 4, **1**	3
2	**0**	1
3	8, 5, 6, **2**	4
4	3, **1**	2
5	9, 7, **0**	3

Average donors needed $= (3 + 1 + 4 + 2 + 3) \div 5 = 2.6$.

Answer: The simulation suggests about 2–3 donors are needed to find one with type A blood.

More trials = better estimates. 10 trials give a rough idea; 100+ trials give reliable results.

Experimental Probability

1. A coin is tossed 100 times. Heads comes up 48 times. What is the experimental probability of heads? How does it compare to the theoretical probability?

2. A spinner has 4 equal sections: red, blue, green, yellow. After 80 spins, red appeared 24 times. Find the experimental probability. Is the spinner fair?

3. Design a simulation to estimate the probability that a family with 3 children has all girls. Describe your model and how to run it.

4. In a simulation, a die is rolled 60 times. A 6 appeared 15 times. What is the experimental probability? What would you expect theoretically?

5. A random-number generator produces digits 0–9. You want to simulate a 40% chance of rain. Which

digits would represent rain? Run 10 trials with: $3, 7, 1, 0, 9, 4, 2, 8, 5, 6$. What experimental probability do you get?

9.4 Probability Models

Learning Goals

- Develop and compare uniform and non-uniform probability models
- Compare predicted probabilities to observed frequencies

Probability Models

- **Uniform model**: All outcomes equally likely
- **Non-uniform model**: Outcomes have different probabilities

Spinner Model

A spinner has 4 equal sections. What is the probability of landing on any section?

Uniform: $1/4$

Answer: $1/4$

TIP
Compare predictions to actual results to check your model.

Probability Models

1. A bag has 2 red, 3 blue, 5 green marbles. Is this a uniform model?
2. A die is rolled. Is this a uniform model?
3. A spinner has 3 sections: 1 large, 2 small. Is this uniform?
4. If a coin is weighted to land heads 70% of the time, is this uniform?
5. Why compare predicted probabilities to observed frequencies?

9.5 Sample Spaces for Compound Events

Learning Goals

- Represent sample spaces using lists, tables, and tree diagrams
- Identify all possible outcomes for compound events

Sample Space

A sample space lists all possible outcomes of an experiment.

Flipping Two Coins

List all possible outcomes.

HH, HT, TH, TT

Answer: HH, HT, TH, TT

TIP

Tree diagrams help organize outcomes for compound events.

Sample Spaces

1. List all outcomes for rolling a die and flipping a coin.
2. List all outcomes for picking a red or blue marble, then flipping a coin.
3. How many outcomes for flipping 3 coins?
4. List all outcomes for rolling two dice.
5. Why use a tree diagram?

9.6 Finding Probabilities of Compound Events

Learning Goals

- Calculate probabilities by counting favorable outcomes in a sample space
- Apply to everyday situations (dice, cards, etc.)

Compound Probability

$P = \frac{\text{favorable outcomes}}{\text{total outcomes}}$

Rolling Two Dice

What is the probability of rolling a sum of 7?

Favorable: $(1,6),(2,5),(3,4),(4,3),(5,2),(6,1)$ (6 out of 36) $P = 6/36 = 1/6$

Answer: $1/6$

TIP
Count all possible outcomes, then count those that fit the event.

Compound Probability

1. What is the probability of flipping two heads in two coin tosses?
2. What is the probability of rolling a 2 and a 3 on two dice?
3. What is the probability of drawing two red marbles from a bag of 5 red and 5 blue (without replacement)?
4. What is the probability of picking a heart and then a spade from a deck (without replacement)?
5. What is the probability of rolling an even number on both dice?

9.7 Simulating Compound Events

Learning Goals

- Design and use simulations to model compound events
- Use random digits to generate frequencies

Simulation

A simulation uses random numbers or physical models to imitate real events.

Simulating Dice Rolls

Simulate rolling two dice 100 times. How many times do you expect a sum of 7?

Probability: $1/6$; Expected: $100 \times 1/6 \approx 17$

Answer: 17 **times**

TIP
Simulations help estimate probabilities when calculations are hard.

Simulating Events

1. Simulate flipping a coin 50 times. How many heads expected?
2. Simulate rolling a die 60 times. How many times expect a 3?
3. Simulate drawing a red marble from a bag (3 red, 7 blue) 40 times. How many reds expected?
4. Simulate picking two cards from a deck 100 times. How many times expect both to be hearts?
5. Simulate rolling two dice 36 times. How many times expect a sum of 2?

Answer Key & Explanations

Check Your Answers

Use each explanation to check the method, not just the final answer.

Chapter 1

Section 1.1

1. 2 walls per hour
2. $\frac{2}{3}$ cup per minute
3. $1\frac{1}{4}$ gallons per mile
4. Equal — both 2 cups per cup
5. Beetle: $\frac{7}{8}$ m/hr $> \frac{5}{6}$ m/hr

Explanations

1. Divide the wall covered by the time: $\frac{2}{3} \div \frac{1}{3}$. Flip the second fraction and multiply: $\frac{2}{3} \times \frac{3}{1} = \frac{6}{3} = 2$ walls per hour.

2. Divide cups by minutes: $\frac{1}{2} \div \frac{3}{4}$. Flip and multiply: $\frac{1}{2} \times \frac{4}{3} = \frac{4}{6} = \frac{2}{3}$ cup per minute.

3. Divide gallons by miles: $\frac{5}{6} \div \frac{2}{3}$. Flip and multiply: $\frac{5}{6} \times \frac{3}{2} = \frac{15}{12} = \frac{5}{4} = 1\frac{1}{4}$ gallons per mile.

4. Find each unit rate. Mix A: $\frac{1}{2} \div \frac{1}{4} = \frac{1}{2} \times 4 = 2$. Mix B: $\frac{2}{3} \div \frac{1}{3} = \frac{2}{3} \times 3 = 2$. Both give 2 cups of nuts per cup of raisins, so they are equal.

5. Find each unit rate. Snail: $\frac{5}{8} \div \frac{3}{4} = \frac{5}{8} \times \frac{4}{3} = \frac{20}{24} = \frac{5}{6}$ m/hr. Beetle: $\frac{7}{10} \div \frac{4}{5} = \frac{7}{10} \times \frac{5}{4} = \frac{35}{40} = \frac{7}{8}$ m/hr. Since $\frac{7}{8} > \frac{5}{6}$, the beetle is faster.

Section 1.2

1 Yes 2 No 3 True 4 Plan 1

Explanations

1 Divide $y \div x$ for each row: $9 \div 3 = 3$, $15 \div 5 = 3$, $21 \div 7 = 3$. Every ratio is 3, so the relationship is proportional.

2 Divide $y \div x$ for each row: $6 \div 2 = 3$, $10 \div 4 = 2.5$, $14 \div 6 \approx 2.3$. The ratios are not all equal, so this is not proportional. It has a constant change of $+4$, but that does not mean a constant ratio.

4 Plan 1 has no base fee, so dividing total cost by texts always gives $\$0.05$. That constant ratio means it is proportional. Plan 2 has a $\$5$ monthly charge that does not depend on texts, so the cost-per-text ratio changes and it is not proportional.

Section 1.3

1 $k = 4$ 2 $k = 60$ miles per hour 3 $k = 2.5$ 4 $k = 16$ pages/min 5 $y = 21$

Explanations

1 Pick any row and divide y by x: $12 \div 3 = 4$. Check another row: $20 \div 5 = 4$ and $32 \div 8 = 4$. All ratios match, so $k = 4$.

2 Divide miles by hours: $30 \div \frac{1}{2} = 30 \times 2 = 60$. This means the car travels 60 miles for every 1 hour. Check: $60 \div 1 = 60$ and $120 \div 2 = 60$ ✓.

3 On a proportional graph, $k = y \div x$. Use the given point: $k = 15 \div 6 = 2.5$. This means y increases by 2.5 for every 1 unit of x.

4 Divide to find the unit rate: $80 \div 5 = 16$. The printer produces 16 pages every minute.

5 First find k: $14 \div 4 = 3.5$. Then use $y = kx$ to find the missing value: $y = 3.5 \times 6 = 21$. Check: $35 \div 10 = 3.5$ ✓.

Section 1.4

1 $c = 8h$ 2 $g = 3.5m$ 3 $y = 2.5x$ 4 9 cups 5 250 texts

Explanations

1 The rate is \$8 per hour, so $k = 8$. Plug into $y = kx$: cost $= 8\times$ hours, giving $c = 8h$.

2 The unit rate is 3.5 gallons per minute, so $k = 3.5$. The equation is $g = 3.5m$.

3 Find k by dividing any y by its x: $10 \div 4 = 2.5$. Check: $15 \div 6 = 2.5$ ✓. Write the equation: $y = 2.5x$.

4 The equation is $f = \frac{3}{4}s$ where s is servings. Plug in 12: $f = \frac{3}{4} \times 12 = \frac{36}{4} = 9$ cups of flour.

5 Write the equation: $c = 0.04t$. Set $c = 10$ and solve: $10 = 0.04t$, so $t = 10 \div 0.04 = 250$ texts.

Section 1.5

1 One ticket costs \$5 | 2 Unit rate $= 6$; $y = 42$ | 3 Runner A | 4 False | 5 $y = 2.5x$; $x = 16$

Explanations

1 The point $(1, r)$ on a proportional graph gives the unit rate. Here $x = 1$ ticket and $y = 5$ dollars, so one ticket costs \$5.

2 Find the unit rate: $k = 18 \div 3 = 6$. This means y increases by 6 for every 1 unit of x. Now plug in $x = 7$: $y = 6 \times 7 = 42$.

3 Find each unit rate. Runner A: $k = 10 \div 2 = 5$ units per time. Runner B: $k = 8 \div 2 = 4$. A higher k means a steeper line and a faster speed, so Runner A is faster.

5 Find k: $12.5 \div 5 = 2.5$, so the equation is $y = 2.5x$. To find x when $y = 40$: $40 = 2.5x$, divide both sides by 2.5: $x = 40 \div 2.5 = 16$.

Section 1.6

1 350 miles | 2 $3\frac{3}{4}$ cups | 3 64 km | 4 30 min | 5 Large by \$2/gal

Explanations

1 Find the unit rate: $210 \div 6 = 35$ miles per gallon. Multiply by 10: $35 \times 10 = 350$ miles.

2 Find rice per person: $\frac{3}{2} \div 4 = \frac{3}{8}$ cup. Multiply by 10: $\frac{3}{8} \times 10 = \frac{30}{8} = 3\frac{3}{4}$ cups.

3 Set up a proportion: $\frac{3}{24} = \frac{8}{d}$. Cross-multiply: $3d = 24 \times 8 = 192$. Divide: $d = 192 \div 3 = 64$ km.

4 Find the unit rate: $120 \div 8 = 15$ pages per minute. Divide: $450 \div 15 = 30$ minutes.

5 Find each unit price. Small: $18 \div 0.75 = \$24$ per gallon. Large: $33 \div 1.5 = \$22$ per gallon. The large can costs $\$2$ less per gallon, so it is the better deal.

Chapter 2

Section 2.1

1 30 2 40% 3 36 4 70% 5 204

Explanations

1 Convert the percent to a decimal: $15\% = 0.15$. Multiply: $0.15 \times 200 = 30$.

2 Divide the part by the whole: $36 \div 90 = 0.4$. Convert to a percent by multiplying by 100. $0.4 \times 100 = 40\%$.

3 You know the part (27) and the percent ($75\% = 0.75$). Divide the part by the percent: $27 \div 0.75 = 36$. Check: $0.75 \times 36 = 27$ ✓.

4 Divide the part by the whole: $42 \div 60 = 0.7$. Multiply by 100 to get the percent: $0.7 \times 100 = 70\%$.

5 Convert 85% to a decimal: 0.85. Multiply by the total: $0.85 \times 240 = 204$ items in stock.

Section 2.2

1 36 2 45% 3 130 4 14% 5 $345.6 \approx 346$ students

Explanations

1 Set up the proportion: $\frac{n}{80} = \frac{45}{100}$. Cross-multiply: $100n = 80 \times 45 = 3600$. Divide both sides by 100: $n = 36$.

2 Set up the proportion with the percent unknown: $\frac{54}{120} = \frac{p}{100}$. Cross-multiply: $120p = 54 \times 100 = 5400$. Divide: $p = 5400 \div 120 = 45$, so 45%.

3 Set up the proportion with the whole unknown: $\frac{78}{w} = \frac{60}{100}$. Cross-multiply: $60w = 78 \times 100 = 7800$. Divide: $w = 7800 \div 60 = 130$.

4 Set up the proportion: $\frac{35}{250} = \frac{p}{100}$. Cross-multiply: $250p = 3500$. Divide: $p = 3500 \div 250 = 14$, so 14% of the marbles are red.

5 Set up: $\frac{n}{480} = \frac{72}{100}$. Cross-multiply: $100n = 480 \times 72 = 34{,}560$. Divide: $n = 345.6$. Round to 346 since you can't have a partial student.

> Section 2.3

1	2	3	4	5
15%	$\$135$	25%	0.60	20%

Explanations

1 First find the change: $9{,}200 - 8{,}000 = 1{,}200$. Divide by the original: $1{,}200 \div 8{,}000 = 0.15$. Multiply by 100: the population increased by 15%.

2 A 25% discount means you pay $100\% - 25\% = 75\%$ of the price. Multiply: $180 \times 0.75 = \$135$.

3 Find the change: $15 - 12 = 3$ cm. Divide by the original height: $3 \div 12 = 0.25$. Multiply by 100: that is a 25% increase.

4 A 40% decrease means you keep $100\% - 40\% = 60\%$. Convert to a decimal: $60\% = 0.60$. Multiply the original by 0.60 to get the result.

5 Find the change: $40 - 32 = 8$. Divide by the original price: $8 \div 40 = 0.2$. Multiply by 100: the price decreased by 20%.

> Section 2.4

1 $21 2 $45.50 3 $23.32 4 $73.44 5 60%

Explanations

1 A 75% markup means the price is $100\% + 75\% = 175\%$ of the cost. Multiply: $12 \times 1.75 = \$21$.

2 A 30% discount means you pay $100\% - 30\% = 70\%$. Multiply: $65 \times 0.70 = \$45.50$.

3 Tax is added on top, so multiply by $1 + 0.06 = 1.06$. Total: $22 \times 1.06 = \$23.32$.

4 First apply the discount: $80 \times 0.85 = \$68$. Then add tax to the sale price: $68 \times 1.08 = \$73.44$. Always apply tax last.

5 Find the markup amount: $40 - 25 = \$15$. Divide by the original cost: $15 \div 25 = 0.60$. Multiply by 100: that is a 60% markup.

Section 2.5

1 $6.30 2 $270 3 $84 4 About $9.30 5 $14,000

Explanations

1 Convert the percent to a decimal: $18\% = 0.18$. Multiply by the bill: $35 \times 0.18 = \$6.30$.

2 Commission means she earns 6% of total sales. Convert: $6\% = 0.06$. Multiply: $4{,}500 \times 0.06 = \$270$.

3 The fee is added on top, so you pay $100\% + 12\% = 112\%$. Multiply: $75 \times 1.12 = \$84$.

4 Find 10% by moving the decimal: $6.20. Find 5% by taking half of that: $3.10. Add them: $6.20 + 3.10 = \$9.30$. That is 15%.

5 Convert the percent: $4\% = 0.04$. Multiply by the sale price: $350{,}000 \times 0.04 = \$14{,}000$.

Section 2.6

1 $80 | 2 $288 | 3 Account B ($50 vs. $45) | 4 4% | 5 4 years

Explanations

1 Use $I = Prt$: $I = 800 \times 0.05 \times 2 = \$80$. This is the money the bank pays you for keeping your savings there.

2 $I = 1{,}200 \times 0.06 \times 4 = \$288$. This is the extra cost of borrowing the money.

3 A: $I = 500 \times 0.03 \times 3 = \$45$. B: $I = 500 \times 0.02 \times 5 = \$50$. Even though B has a lower rate, the longer time makes it earn $\$5$ more.

4 Solve for r: $240 = 2{,}000 \times r \times 3$. So $6{,}000r = 240$ and $r = 0.04 = 4\%$.

5 Solve for t: $150 = 1{,}500 \times 0.025 \times t$. So $37.5t = 150$ and $t = 4$ years.

Section 2.7

1 20% | 2 20% | 3 ≈ 6.7% | 4 ≈ 8.7% | 5 True

Explanations

1 Find the difference: $|30 - 25| = 5$. Divide by the actual value: $5 \div 25 = 0.2$. Multiply by 100: the percent error is 20%.

2 Find the difference: $|2 - 2.5| = 0.5$. Divide by the actual: $0.5 \div 2.5 = 0.2$. Multiply by 100: 20% error. The absolute value makes the answer positive even though the estimate was too low.

3 Find the difference: $|3.2 - 3| = 0.2$. Divide by the actual: $0.2 \div 3 = 0.0\overline{6}$. Multiply by 100: about 6.7% error.

4 Find the difference: $|5{,}000 - 4{,}600| = 400$. Divide by the actual value: $400 \div 4{,}600 \approx 0.087$. Multiply by 100: about 8.7% error.

Section 2.8

1 $22.50 | 2 $15 more | 3 False | 4 Advantage: buy now; Disadvantage: interest charges

5 \$36

Explanations

1 $I = 150 \times 0.15 \times 1 = \$22.50$.

2 Bank A: $1{,}000 \times 0.02 = \$20$. Bank B: $1{,}000 \times 0.035 = \$35$. Difference: $35 - 20 = \$15$.

4 Credit lets you purchase before you have the cash, but you pay interest if you don't pay the full balance on time.

5 Bank fee per year: $5 \times 12 = \$60$. Credit union: $2 \times 12 = \$24$. Savings: $60 - 24 = \$36$.

Section 2.9

1 \$300 2 \$9 3 \$150/month 4 6.25% 5 Savings: safe; Investment: higher growth

Explanations

1 $2{,}000 - 1{,}100 - 600 = \$300$.

2 Total saved: $50 \times 12 = \$600$. Average balance over a year is about \$300, but simple interest on \$600 for half a year averages out. Approximate: $I = 600 \times 0.03 \times 0.5 = \$9$.

3 Divide: $1{,}200 \div 8 = \$150$ per month.

4 Over by \$25. Percent: $25 \div 400 = 0.0625 = 6.25\%$.

5 Savings accounts are low-risk — your money is safe. Investments can grow faster but carry the risk of losing value.

Section 2.10

1 \$1,102.50 2 Simple: \$240; Compound: \$242 3 \$899.89 4 You earn interest on your interest

5 \$699.84

Explanations

1. Year 1: $1{,}000 \times 1.05 = \$1{,}050$. Year 2: $1{,}050 \times 1.05 = \$1{,}102.50$.

2. Simple: $I = 200 \times 0.10 \times 2 = \$40$; total $= \$240$. Compound: $200 \times 1.10 = 220$; $220 \times 1.10 = \$242$.

3. $A = 800(1.04)^3 = 800 \times 1.124864 = \$899.89$ (rounded to the nearest cent).

4. With compound interest, each year the base grows because previous interest is added. Simple interest always uses the original principal.

5. Year 1: $600 \times 1.08 = \$648$. Year 2: $648 \times 1.08 = \$699.84$.

Chapter 3

Section 3.1

1. 8 2. 12 and 7 3. 0 yards 4. False 5. $-7, -4, 0, 2, 5$

Explanations

1. The opposite of a negative number is positive. -8 is 8 units left of 0, so its opposite is 8 units right of 0.

2. Absolute value measures distance from 0. -12 is 12 units from 0, so $|-12| = 12$. 7 is 7 units from 0, so $|7| = 7$.

3. Gain $= +6$, loss $= -6$. Add: $6 + (-6) = 0$. The team is back where it started because the gain and loss are opposites.

5. On a number line, numbers increase from left to right. -7 is farthest left, then -4, then 0, then 2, then 5.

Section 3.2

1 -13 2 -5 3 0 4 $8°C$ 5 -7

Explanations

1 Both are negative, so add the absolute values: $8+5=13$. Keep the negative sign: -13.

2 Different signs, so subtract: $12-7=5$. The larger absolute value is 12 (negative), so the answer is -5.

3 These are opposites (additive inverses). A number plus its opposite always equals 0.

4 Start at -6 and add 14: $(-6)+14=8$. Different signs, so subtract $14-6=8$, and the larger absolute value is positive.

5 First add the negatives: $(-9)+(-4)=-13$. Then add 6: $(-13)+6=-7$. Subtract $13-6=7$, keep the negative sign.

> Section 3.3

1 -6 2 5 3 $-13°C$ 4 13 units 5 2

Explanations

1 Rewrite as adding the opposite: $10+(-16)$. Different signs, so subtract: $16-10=6$. The larger absolute value is negative, so the answer is -6.

2 Rewrite: $(-7)+12$. Different signs, so $12-7=5$. The larger absolute value is positive, so the answer is 5.

3 Subtract: $-8-5=-8+(-5)=-13$. The temperature dropped 13 degrees.

4 Distance $=|-9-4|=|-13|=13$. You can also count: from -9 to 0 is 9 units, then 0 to 4 is 4 units, total 13.

5 Rewrite both subtractions: $(-3)+(-5)+10$. Add the negatives first: $-3+(-5)=-8$. Then add 10: $-8+10=2$.

> Section 3.4

1 -1.7 2 $-\frac{5}{4}$ or $-1\frac{1}{4}$ 3 -2.5 4 $\frac{7}{6}$ or $1\frac{1}{6}$ 5 -10.9 m

Explanations

1 Different signs, so subtract the absolute values: $3.5 - 1.8 = 1.7$. The larger absolute value (3.5) is negative, so the answer is -1.7.

2 Rewrite subtraction as addition: $-\frac{1}{2} + (-\frac{3}{4})$. Common denominator 4: $-\frac{2}{4} + (-\frac{3}{4})$. Same signs, add: $\frac{2+3}{4} = \frac{5}{4}$. Both negative, so $-\frac{5}{4}$.

3 Different signs, so subtract: $6.7 - 4.2 = 2.5$. The larger absolute value (6.7) is negative, so the answer is -2.5.

4 Subtracting a negative means add: $\frac{5}{6} + \frac{1}{3}$. Common denominator 6: $\frac{5}{6} + \frac{2}{6} = \frac{7}{6} = 1\frac{1}{6}$.

5 Start at -12.5. Go up: $-12.5 + 4.8 = -7.7$. Go down: $-7.7 + (-3.2) = -10.9$ m.

Section 3.5

1 54 2 -28 3 $\frac{3}{10}$ 4 -0.6 5 -30

Explanations

1 Multiply the absolute values: $6 \times 9 = 54$. Same signs (both negative) give a positive result: 54.

2 Multiply the absolute values: $4 \times 7 = 28$. Different signs (one negative, one positive) give a negative result: -28.

3 Multiply numerators: $3 \times 2 = 6$. Multiply denominators: $4 \times 5 = 20$. Both negative ☒ positive: $\frac{6}{20} = \frac{3}{10}$.

4 Multiply the absolute values: $1.5 \times 0.4 = 0.6$. Different signs ☒ negative: -0.6.

5 Multiply in steps: $(-2) \times (-3) = 6$ (same signs ☒ positive). Then $6 \times (-5) = -30$ (different signs ☒ negative). Three negatives (odd count) give a negative product.

Section 3.6

1 8 2 -5 3 $-\frac{5}{2}$ or $-2\frac{1}{2}$ 4 -4 5 -30 m/min

Explanations

1 Divide the absolute values: $48 \div 6 = 8$. Same signs (both negative) give a positive result: 8.

2 Divide the absolute values: $35 \div 7 = 5$. Different signs ⊠ negative: -5.

3 Flip and multiply: $\frac{5}{6} \times \frac{3}{1} = \frac{15}{6} = \frac{5}{2}$. Different signs ⊠ negative: $-\frac{5}{2}$.

4 Divide the absolute values: $4.8 \div 1.2 = 4$. Different signs ⊠ negative: -4.

5 Descending means negative depth: $-240 \div 8 = -30$. The submarine goes down 30 meters each minute.

Section 3.7

1 0.875 2 $0.\overline{4}$ 3 $0.\overline{45}$ 4 False 5 $-0.58\overline{3}$

Explanations

1 Divide $7 \div 8$: 8 goes into 70 eight times (64), remainder 6. 8 into 60 seven times (56), remainder 4. 8 into 40 five times (40), remainder 0. So $\frac{7}{8} = 0.875$ (terminates).

2 Divide $4 \div 9 = 0.444\ldots$ The remainder keeps being 4, so the digit 4 repeats forever. Write $0.\overline{4}$.

3 Divide $5 \div 11 = 0.454545\ldots$ The pattern 45 repeats. Write $0.\overline{45}$.

5 Divide $7 \div 12 = 0.5833\ldots$ The digit 3 repeats after 58. Add the negative sign: $-0.58\overline{3}$.

Section 3.8

1 $\$41.70$ 2 $1\frac{7}{12}$ cups 3 6 yards 4 $\$14.65$ 5 $-5\frac{1}{2}$

Explanations

1 Add each change in order: $42.30 + 1.75 = 44.05$. Then $44.05 - 3.20 = 40.85$. Then $40.85 + 0.85 = 41.70$.

2 Subtract: $2\frac{1}{4} - \frac{2}{3} = \frac{9}{4} - \frac{2}{3}$. Common denominator 12: $\frac{27}{12} - \frac{8}{12} = \frac{19}{12} = 1\frac{7}{12}$ cups of water.

3 Add all changes: $3 + (-7) + 12 + (-2)$. Group positives: $3 + 12 = 15$. Group negatives: $(-7) + (-2) = -9$. Combine: $15 + (-9) = 6$ yards gained.

4 Divide the bill: $48.60 \div 4 = \$12.15$ per person. Add the tip: $12.15 + 2.50 = \$14.65$.

5 Multiply first: $-\frac{1}{2} \times 8 = -4$. Divide: $\frac{3}{4} \div (-\frac{1}{2}) = \frac{3}{4} \times (-2) = -\frac{3}{2}$. Add: $-4 + (-\frac{3}{2}) = -\frac{8}{2} + (-\frac{3}{2}) = -\frac{11}{2} = -5\frac{1}{2}$.

Chapter 4

Section 4.1

1 $3n - 8$ 2 -1 3 -1 4 $0.10t + 15$ 5 $\$23.50$

Explanations

1 "3 times a number" is $3n$. "8 less than" means subtract 8 from that result: $3n - 8$.

2 Substitute: $4(-2) + 7 = -8 + 7 = -1$.

3 Substitute: $\frac{12}{3} - 5 = 4 - 5 = -1$.

4 Each text costs $\$0.10$, so t texts cost $0.10t$. Add the $\$15$ fee: $0.10t + 15$.

5 Substitute $t = 85$: $0.10(85) + 15 = 8.50 + 15 = \$23.50$.

Section 4.2

1. $8a - 3$
2. $8x - 5$
3. $4y - 3$
4. $\frac{5}{4}n - 2$ or $1\frac{1}{4}n - 2$
5. False

Explanations

1. $6a$ and $2a$ are like terms: $6a + 2a = 8a$. The -3 has no like term, so the result is $8a - 3$.
2. Group like terms: $(5x + 3x) + (-9 + 4) = 8x + (-5) = 8x - 5$.
3. Combine variable terms: $-2y + 6y = 4y$. Combine constants: $7 + (-10) = -3$. Result: $4y - 3$.
4. Find a common denominator for the coefficients: $\frac{2}{4}n + \frac{3}{4}n = \frac{5}{4}n$. The constant stays: $\frac{5}{4}n - 2$.

Section 4.3

1. $10x + 15$
2. $-12a + 6$
3. $3x - 5$
4. $10x + 2$
5. $4x + 13$

Explanations

1. Multiply 5 by each term inside: $5 \times 2x = 10x$ and $5 \times 3 = 15$. Result: $10x + 15$.
2. Multiply -3 by each term: $-3 \times 4a = -12a$ and $-3 \times (-2) = +6$. A negative times a negative is positive.
3. Multiply $\frac{1}{2}$ by each term: $\frac{1}{2} \times 6x = 3x$ and $\frac{1}{2} \times (-10) = -5$. Result: $3x - 5$.
4. First expand: $2(3x + 1) = 6x + 2$. Then combine like terms: $6x + 2 + 4x = 10x + 2$.
5. Expand each part: $-2x + 10 + 6x + 3$. Combine like terms: $(-2x + 6x) + (10 + 3) = 4x + 13$.

Section 4.4

1 $5(2x+5)$ 2 $6(2y-3)$ 3 $7(2a+3b)$ 4 $-3(3x+2)$ 5 False

Explanations

1 The GCF of 10 and 25 is 5. Divide each term: $10x \div 5 = 2x$ and $25 \div 5 = 5$. Write: $5(2x+5)$.

2 The GCF of 12 and 18 is 6. Divide: $12y \div 6 = 2y$ and $-18 \div 6 = -3$. Write: $6(2y-3)$.

3 The GCF of 14 and 21 is 7. Divide: $14a \div 7 = 2a$ and $21b \div 7 = 3b$. Write: $7(2a+3b)$.

4 The GCF is 3. Factor out -3: $-9x \div (-3) = 3x$ and $-6 \div (-3) = 2$. Write: $-3(3x+2)$. Check: $-3(3x+2) = -9x-6$ ✓.

Section 4.5

1 $7x+4$ 2 $5n-12$ 3 10 4 $5x-4$ 5 $6x+2$

Explanations

1 Remove parentheses: $4x+6+3x-2$. Combine like terms: $(4x+3x)+(6-2) = 7x+4$.

2 Distribute the negative: $8n-5-3n-7$. Combine: $(8n-3n)+(-5-7) = 5n-12$.

3 Distribute the negative: $2y+9-2y+1$. The variable terms cancel: $0y+10 = 10$. The answer is just a constant.

4 Combine: $(-x+6x)+(4-8) = 5x-4$.

5 Add all three sides: $(2x+1)+(3x-4)+(x+5)$. Combine: $(2x+3x+x)+(1-4+5) = 6x+2$.

Section 4.6

1 $1.08x$; an 8% increase 2 $p-0.15p$ and $0.85p$ 3 $x+12$ 4 $40h+50$

5 $1.25p \times 0.80 = 1.00p = p$

Explanations

1 Factor out x: $x(1+0.08) = 1.08x$. This means the total is 108% of the original — like adding 8% sales tax.

2 The discount is $0.15p$. Subtract: $p - 0.15p$. Factor: $p(1 - 0.15) = 0.85p$. Both give the same sale price.

3 Expand: $3x + 12 - 2x$. Combine like terms: $(3x - 2x) + 12 = x + 12$.

4 Hourly pay for 40 hours is $40h$. Add the bonus: $40h + 50$. This is already simplified since $40h$ and 50 are not like terms.

5 Increase by 25%: multiply by 1.25. Then decrease by 20%: multiply by 0.80. Combined: $1.25 \times 0.80 = 1.00$, so the final price equals the original p.

Chapter 5

Section 5.1

1 $3n + 7 = 22$ 2 $2.50m + 3 = 18$ 3 $60 - 8w = 12$ 4 $0.05t + 15 = 21.50$ 5 $5n - 9 = 31$

Explanations

1 Each notebook costs \$3, so n notebooks cost $3n$. Add the binder: $3n + 7$. Set equal to the total: $3n + 7 = 22$.

2 The per-mile charge is $2.50m$. Add the base fare: $2.50m + 3$. Set equal to the total cost: $2.50m + 3 = 18$.

3 Start with \$60 and subtract \$8 each week: $60 - 8w$. You want \$12 left: $60 - 8w = 12$.

4 Text cost: $0.05t$. Add monthly fee: $0.05t + 15$. Set equal to bill: $0.05t + 15 = 21.50$.

5 "Five times a number" is $5n$. "Minus 9" gives $5n - 9$. "Equals 31" gives $5n - 9 = 31$.

Section 5.2

1. $x = 8$ 2. $n = 9$ 3. $y = 24$ 4. $x = 4$ 5. 6 months

Explanations

1. Subtract 9 from both sides: $2x = 16$. Divide both sides by 2: $x = 8$. Check: $2(8) + 9 = 25$ ✓.

2. Add 12 to both sides: $5n = 45$. Divide by 5: $n = 9$. Check: $5(9) - 12 = 45 - 12 = 33$ ✓.

3. Subtract 7: $\frac{y}{3} = 8$. Multiply both sides by 3: $y = 24$. Check: $\frac{24}{3} + 7 = 8 + 7 = 15$ ✓.

4. Subtract 10: $-4x = -16$. Divide by -4: $x = 4$. Check: $-4(4) + 10 = -16 + 10 = -6$ ✓.

5. Equation: $10m + 25 = 85$. Subtract 25: $10m = 60$. Divide by 10: $m = 6$. Check: $10(6) + 25 = 85$ ✓.

Section 5.3

1. $x = 4$ 2. $n = 1$ 3. $y = -9$ 4. $x = 4$ 5. $x = 10$

Explanations

1. Divide both sides by 2: $x + 5 = 9$. Subtract 5: $x = 4$. Check: $2(4 + 5) = 2(9) = 18$ ✓.

2. Divide both sides by 5: $n - 3 = -2$. Add 3: $n = 1$. Check: $5(1 - 3) = 5(-2) = -10$ ✓.

3. Divide by -3: $y + 4 = -5$. Subtract 4: $y = -9$. Check: $-3(-9 + 4) = -3(-5) = 15$ ✓.

4. Distribute: $12x - 6 = 42$. Add 6: $12x = 48$. Divide by 12: $x = 4$. Check: $6(2 \cdot 4 - 1) = 6(7) = 42$ ✓.

5. Perimeter $= 4(x + 3) = 52$. Divide by 4: $x + 3 = 13$. Subtract 3: $x = 10$. Each side is 13 cm.

Section 5.4

1 $x = 10$ 2 $x = 17$ 3 $y = 8$ 4 $n = 10$ 5 $24

Explanations

1 Subtract 2.1: $0.3x = 3.0$. Divide by 0.3: $x = 10$. Check: $0.3(10) + 2.1 = 3 + 2.1 = 5.1$ ✓.

2 Multiply every term by 4: $x + 3 = 20$. Subtract 3: $x = 17$. Check: $\frac{17}{4} + \frac{3}{4} = \frac{20}{4} = 5$ ✓.

3 Subtract 4: $-1.5y = -12$. Divide by -1.5: $y = 8$. Check: $-1.5(8) + 4 = -12 + 4 = -8$ ✓.

4 Add 5: $\frac{3n}{2} = 15$. Multiply by 2: $3n = 30$. Divide by 3: $n = 10$. Check: $\frac{3(10)}{2} - 5 = 15 - 5 = 10$ ✓.

5 Let p = original. After markdown: $p - \frac{p}{3} = \frac{2p}{3}$. After \$4 off: $\frac{2p}{3} - 4 = 12$. Add 4: $\frac{2p}{3} = 16$. Multiply by $\frac{3}{2}$: $p = 24$.

Section 5.5

1 $x > 6$ 2 $n \geq 3$ 3 More than 6 days 4 $x \geq 20$ 5 At least 13 questions

Explanations

1 Subtract 5: $2x > 12$. Divide by 2: $x > 6$. Any number greater than 6 is a solution.

2 Subtract 9: $-3n \leq -9$. Divide by -3 and flip the sign: $n \geq 3$.

3 Equation: $50 - 6d < 14$. Subtract 50: $-6d < -36$. Divide by -6 and flip: $d > 6$. After more than 6 days.

4 Add 2: $\frac{x}{4} \geq 5$. Multiply by 4: $x \geq 20$.

5 Inequality: $5q + 15 \geq 80$. Subtract 15: $5q \geq 65$. Divide by 5: $q \geq 13$.

> Section 5.6

1. $x \geq 3$; closed circle at 3, shade right
2. $n > 2$; open circle at 2, shade right
3. $x \geq -4$; closed circle at -4, shade right
4. False
5. $h \leq 6\frac{2}{3}$; closed circle at $6\frac{2}{3}$, shade left

Explanations

1. Subtract 4: $x \geq 3$. Since it includes 3 ("or equal to"), use a closed circle at 3 and shade to the right.
2. Add 6: $3n > 6$. Divide by 3: $n > 2$. Strictly greater than 2, so use an open circle at 2 and shade right.
3. Divide by -2 and flip the sign: $x \geq -4$. Closed circle at -4, shade right.
5. Inequality: $3h \leq 20$. Divide by 3: $h \leq \frac{20}{3} = 6\frac{2}{3}$. You can park at most $6\frac{2}{3}$ hours. Closed circle at $6\frac{2}{3}$, shade left toward 0.

Chapter 6

> Section 6.1

1. 20 ft
2. 15 km per cm
3. 144 inches or 12 ft
4. 96 m^2
5. False

Explanations

1. Multiply drawing length by scale factor: $2.5 \times 8 = 20$ ft.
2. Divide to find the unit rate: $45 \div 3 = 15$. Each centimeter on the map represents 15 km in real life.
3. Multiply by the scale factor: $6 \times 24 = 144$ inches. Convert: $144 \div 12 = 12$ feet.
4. Actual dimensions: $2 \times 4 = 8$ m and $3 \times 4 = 12$ m. Area: $8 \times 12 = 96$ m^2.

Section 6.2

1. 8 cm
2. 6 cm
3. 3 cm
4. 96 cm^2
5. False

Explanations

1. Scale ratio: $\frac{50}{25} = 2$. New length: $4 \times 2 = 8$ cm. The new scale is more detailed, so the drawing gets bigger.
2. Scale ratio: $\frac{100}{50} = 2$. New length: $3 \times 2 = 6$ cm.
3. Scale ratio: $\frac{2}{6} = \frac{1}{3}$. New length: $9 \times \frac{1}{3} = 3$ cm. A smaller scale means a smaller drawing.
4. Scale ratio: $\frac{10}{5} = 2$. New dimensions: $4 \times 2 = 8$ cm by $6 \times 2 = 12$ cm. New area: $8 \times 12 = 96$ cm^2.

Section 6.3

1. No
2. Yes — exactly one (equilateral)
3. Many
4. Exactly one
5. False

Explanations

1. Check: $4 + 6 = 10$, but $10 < 11$. The two shorter sides can't reach each other, so no triangle exists.
2. All three sums pass: $5 + 5 = 10 > 5$ ✓. Three equal sides make exactly one equilateral triangle.
3. The sides must add to 10 (half the perimeter). Possible pairs: 1×9, 2×8, 3×7, etc. Many rectangles satisfy this condition.
4. Two sides and the angle between them (SAS) fully determine a triangle. There is only one right triangle with legs 6 and 8.

Section 6.4

1. The angles work, but the triangle is not unique
2. Yes, unique
3. Yes, unique
4. No

5 $70°$

Explanations

1 $35 + 65 + 80 = 180° ✓$. However, three angles (AAA) allow many triangles of different sizes but the same shape.

2 Check: $7 + 10 = 17 > 15 ✓$, $7 + 15 = 22 > 10 ✓$, $10 + 15 = 25 > 7 ✓$. Three valid sides (SSS) give exactly one triangle.

3 Two sides and the angle between them (SAS) always produce exactly one triangle. This is a right triangle with legs 3 and 4.

4 $90 + 90 + 0 = 180°$, but an angle of $0°$ means the sides collapse into a line. Every angle must be greater than $0°$.

5 $180° - 40° - 70° = 70°$. The third angle is $70°$, making this triangle isosceles (two equal angles).

Section 6.5

1 Rectangle
2 A smaller rectangle
3 A rectangle or a triangle
4 True
5 A circle

Explanations

1 A horizontal cut parallel to the base of a rectangular prism always produces a rectangle the same size and shape as the base.

2 A horizontal cut of a rectangular pyramid parallel to the base gives a rectangle. It is smaller than the base because the pyramid narrows toward the top.

3 Depending on the exact angle, a diagonal slice through a cube can create a rectangle, a triangle, or even a hexagon. One common diagonal gives a rectangle.

5 A cone has a circular base. A horizontal cut parallel to the base is a smaller circle. The higher you cut, the smaller the circle.

Section 6.6

1 $55°$
2 $52°$
3 $x = 10$; angles are $45°$
4 $36°$ and $54°$
5 $80°$ and $100°$

Explanations

1 Complementary angles sum to 90°. Subtract: $90° - 35° = 55°$.

2 Supplementary angles sum to 180°. Subtract: $180° - 128° = 52°$.

3 Vertical angles are equal: $4x + 5 = 6x - 15$. Subtract $4x$: $5 = 2x - 15$. Add 15: $20 = 2x$. Divide: $x = 10$. Angle: $4(10) + 5 = 45°$.

4 Let the angles be $2x$ and $3x$. They sum to 90°: $2x + 3x = 90$, so $5x = 90$ and $x = 18$. Angles: $2(18) = 36°$ and $3(18) = 54°$.

5 $x + 30 + 2x = 180$. Combine: $3x + 30 = 180$. Subtract 30: $3x = 150$. Divide: $x = 50$. Angles: $50 + 30 = 80°$ and $2(50) = 100°$.

Section 6.7

1 15 2 3 3 20 ft 4 $TU = 6, SU = 8$ 5 15 in.

Explanations

1 Scale factor: $\frac{10}{4} = 2.5$. $FG = 6 \times 2.5 = 15$.

2 $15 \div 5 = 3$. The larger triangle is 3 times the smaller.

3 Set up: $\frac{5}{3} = \frac{h}{12}$. Cross-multiply: $3h = 60$. Divide: $h = 20$ ft.

4 Scale: $\frac{4}{10} = 0.4$. $TU = 15 \times 0.4 = 6$. $SU = 20 \times 0.4 = 8$.

5 Scale: $\frac{10}{4} = 2.5$. Long side: $6 \times 2.5 = 15$ in.

Chapter 7

Section 7.1

1 5 cm

2 14 in

3 Center, radius, diameter, circumference

4 3.1

5 Diameter 8 m, circumference 25.12 m

Explanations

1 Radius is half the diameter: $10 \div 2 = 5$ cm.

2 Diameter is twice the radius: $7 \times 2 = 14$ in.

3 Identify each part by its definition and location.

4 π = circumference ÷ diameter $= 31.4 \div 10 = 3.14$. Rounded: 3.1.

5 Diameter: $4 \times 2 = 8$ m. Circumference: $2 \times 3.14 \times 4 = 25.12$ m.

Section 7.2

1 56.52 m

2 47.1 in

3 10 cm

4 37.68 ft

5 2.2 m

Explanations

1 $C = 2\pi r = 2 \times 3.14 \times 9 = 56.52$ m.

2 $C = \pi d = 3.14 \times 15 = 47.1$ in.

3 $d = C/\pi = 31.4/3.14 = 10$ cm.

4 $C = 2\pi r = 2 \times 3.14 \times 6 = 37.68$ ft.

5 $C = \pi d = 3.14 \times 0.7 = 2.198$ m, rounded to 2.2 m.

Section 7.3

1. 201.06 m^2
2. 78.5 in^2
3. 4 cm
4. 28.26 ft^2
5. 113.04 in^2

Explanations

1. $A = \pi r^2 = 3.14 \times 8^2 = 3.14 \times 64 = 201.06$ m^2.
2. Radius is 5 in. $A = 3.14 \times 5^2 = 78.5$ in^2.
3. $A = \pi r^2$. $r^2 = 50.24/3.14 = 16$, so $r = 4$ cm.
4. $A = 3.14 \times 3^2 = 3.14 \times 9 = 28.26$ ft^2.
5. Radius is 6 in. $A = 3.14 \times 6^2 = 113.04$ in^2.

Section 7.4

1. 32 m^2
2. 34.825 in^2
3. 47 ft^2
4. 15.57 cm^2
5. 21 m^2

Explanations

1. Rectangle: $8 \times 3 = 24$ m^2. Triangle: $0.5 \times 8 \times 2 = 8$ m^2. Total: $24 + 8 = 32$ m^2.
2. Square: 25 in^2. Quarter circle: $0.25 \times 3.14 \times 25 = 19.625$ in^2. Total: $25 + 19.625 = 44.625$ in^2.
3. Rectangle: $10 \times 4 = 40$ ft^2. Triangle: $0.5 \times 10 \times 3 = 15$ ft^2. Total: $40 + 15 = 55$ ft^2.
4. Rectangle: $7 \times 2 = 14$ cm^2. Semicircle: $0.5 \times 3.14 \times 1^2 = 1.57$ cm^2. Total: $14 + 1.57 = 15.57$ cm^2.
5. First: $5 \times 3 = 15$ m^2. Second: $2 \times 3 = 6$ m^2. Total: $15 + 6 = 21$ m^2.

Section 7.5

1. $150\ m^2$ 2. $74\ in^2$ 3. $88\ ft^2$ 4. $134\ cm^2$ 5. $192\ m^2$

Explanations

1. Cube has 6 faces: $6 \times 5^2 = 6 \times 25 = 150$ m^2.
2. $2(7 \times 2) + 2(7 \times 3) + 2(2 \times 3) = 28 + 42 + 12 = 82$ in^2.
3. $2(6 \times 4) + 2(6 \times 2) + 2(4 \times 2) = 48 + 24 + 16 = 88$ ft^2.
4. Base: $8 \times 3 = 24$ cm^2. Sides: $2 \times 8 \times 5 = 80$ cm^2, $2 \times 3 \times 5 = 30$ cm^2. Total: $24 + 80 + 30 = 134$ cm^2.
5. Base: $0.5 \times 6 \times 4 = 12$ m^2. Sides: $6 \times 10 = 60$ m^2, $4 \times 10 = 40$ m^2, $5 \times 10 = 50$ m^2. Total: $12 + 60 + 40 + 50 = 162$ m^2.

Section 7.6

1. $64\ m^3$ 2. $60\ in^3$ 3. $48\ ft^3$ 4. $84\ cm^3$ 5. $180\ m^3$

Explanations

1. Cube: $4^3 = 64$ m^3.
2. Base: $6 \times 2 = 12$ in^2. Height: 5 in. $V = 12 \times 5 = 60$ in^3.
3. Base: $8 \times 3 = 24$ ft^2. Height: 2 ft. $V = 24 \times 2 = 48$ ft^3.
4. Base: $7 \times 2 = 14$ cm^2. Height: 6 cm. $V = 14 \times 6 = 84$ cm^3.
5. Base: $0.5 \times 5 \times 3 = 7.5$ m^2. Length: 12 m. $V = 7.5 \times 12 = 90$ m^3.

Chapter 8

Section 8.1

1. No — it is biased
2. Population: 5,000 bulbs; sample: 50 bulbs
3. Question, population, method, collect, analyze
4. It avoids bias
5. Biased sample

Explanations

1. Students who arrive early may have different homework habits than others. A better method is to randomly select 10 names from the class list.

2. The factory uses the sample to estimate the quality of the whole batch without testing every single bulb.

3. 1) Question: Which lunch is most popular? 2) Population: all students. 3) Method: randomly select 50 students. 4) Collect: survey their lunch choice. 5) Analyze: tally results and find the most common choice.

4. Random sampling gives every member an equal chance of being selected, so the sample is more likely to represent the whole population accurately.

5. Employees may have opinions influenced by loyalty or job concerns. The population of interest is all potential customers, not just employees.

Section 8.2

1. 15 cm (estimate)
2. Random variation
3. Population mean is likely between 20 and 22
4. Use larger or more samples
5. Biased prediction

Explanations

1. The sample mean is a good estimate for the population mean.

2 Each sample may include different members, causing variation.

3 Multiple samples help narrow down the estimate.

4 More data reduces the effect of random variation.

5 Non-random samples may not represent the population, leading to inaccurate predictions.

Section 8.3

1 Second class
2 Some members of each group are similar
3 Shows how spread out the data is
4 Group A is more spread out
5 Average distance from the mean

Explanations

1 The mean of 85 is higher than 80.

2 Overlap means not all members are different.

3 Variability helps understand differences beyond just the mean.

4 A larger range means more variability.

5 MAD measures variability in a data set.

Section 8.4

1 Group A
2 Y averages slightly more but is much less consistent
3 IQR ignores outliers
4 Range $= 45$; IQR $= 10$; IQR is better
5 Class A

Explanations

1 Group A has a smaller range (20 vs. 40) and smaller IQR (8 vs. 18), meaning its data is more tightly clustered around the center.

2 Student Y's IQR is nearly triple Student X's, meaning Y's daily steps vary much more. X is more consistent day to day.

3 Range uses only the two extreme values, which can be misleading if there is an outlier. IQR measures the spread of the middle 50% and gives a more stable comparison.

4 Range: $50 - 5 = 45$. $Q_1 = 8$, $Q_3 = 18$, so IQR $= 10$. The outlier 50 inflates the range. IQR shows the typical spread more accurately.

5 Class A has a higher median (82 vs. 78) and a smaller IQR (6 vs. 14), meaning most students scored close to 82. Class B is both lower and more spread out.

Section 8.5

1 Stems $1, 2, 3$; Leaves: $5\ 8$, $2\ 5\ 7$, $1\ 3\ 8$ 2 51 3 23 4 9 values 5 True

Explanations

1 Split each number: stem 1: leaves $5, 8$; stem 2: leaves $2, 5, 7$; stem 3: leaves $1, 3, 8$.

2 Data: $41, 43, 45, 50, 52, 57, 58, 64$. Eight values. Median $= \frac{50+52}{2} = 51$.

3 Range $= 64 - 41 = 23$.

4 Count the leaves: $3 + 4 + 2 = 9$.

Section 8.6

1 150 people 2 $90°$ 3 20% 4 30% 5 20%

Explanations

1. $500 \times 0.30 = 150.$

2. $\frac{1}{4} \times 360° = 90°.$

3. Total must be 100%: $35 + 25 + 20 + x = 100$. So $x = 20\%$.

4. $\frac{12}{40} = 0.30 = 30\%.$

5. $\frac{72}{360} = 0.20 = 20\%.$

Chapter 9

Section 9.1

1 0.5 | 2 0.3 | 3 Certain event | 4 Impossible event | 5 Equally likely or not

Explanations

1. There are 2 outcomes, heads and tails. $1/2 = 0.5$.

2. There are 10 marbles, 3 are red. $3/10 = 0.3$.

3. Probability 1 means the event will always happen.

4. Probability 0 means the event cannot happen.

5. The event is just as likely to happen as not.

Section 9.2

1. $1/4$
2. 0.5
3. 0.25
4. $2/13$
5. $1/3$

Explanations

1. There are 13 hearts out of 52 cards. $13/52 = 1/4$.
2. Even numbers: $2, 4, 6$ (3 out of 6). $3/6 = 0.5$.
3. 5 out of 20 marbles. $5/20 = 0.25$.
4. Each suit has 1 of each, so 2 out of 13 per suit.
5. Numbers 5 and 6 (2 out of 6). $2/6 = 1/3$.

Section 9.3

1. 0.48; close to the theoretical 0.50
2. 0.30; slightly above 0.25 but likely fair
3. Use a coin; H = boy, T = girl; flip 3 times per trial
4. 0.25; theoretical is $\frac{1}{6} \approx 0.167$
5. Rain = digits 0–3; experimental $P = 0.40$

Explanations

1. $P = 48 \div 100 = 0.48$. The theoretical probability is 0.50. The small difference is expected — with more tosses, the experimental value would get closer to 0.50.
2. $P = 24 \div 80 = 0.30$. Theoretical $= 0.25$. The small difference could be due to chance in 80 trials. More spins would help confirm.
3. Each child is equally likely to be a boy or girl — like a coin flip. Flip 3 coins per trial. Record how many trials give 3 tails (all girls). Repeat $50+$ trials. Divide all-girl trials by total trials.
4. $P = 15 \div 60 = 0.25$. Theoretical $= \frac{1}{6} \approx 0.167$. The experimental value is noticeably higher — this could be chance, or the die may not be fair.

5 40% $= 4$ out of 10 digits. Choose $0, 1, 2, 3$ for rain. In the 10 trials: rain digits are $3, 1, 0, 2$ — that's 4 rain events. $P = 4 \div 10 = 0.40$.

Section 9.4

1 No 2 Yes 3 No 4 No 5 To check model accuracy

Explanations

1 Probabilities are different for each color.

2 Each number 1–6 is equally likely.

3 Sections are not equal, so probabilities differ.

4 Probabilities are not equal for heads and tails.

5 If results differ, the model may need adjustment.

Section 9.5

1 $6 \times 2 = 12$ outcomes 2 4 outcomes 3 8 outcomes 4 36 outcomes

5 To organize outcomes

Explanations

1 Each die roll (1–6) with heads or tails: $1H, 1T, 2H, 2T, ..., 6T$.

2 Red-Head, Red-Tail, Blue-Head, Blue-Tail.

3 $2^3 = 8$; HHH, HHT, HTH, HTT, THH, THT, TTH, TTT.

4 $6 \times 6 = 36$; each die has 6 options.

5 Tree diagrams show all possible paths for compound events.

Section 9.6

1 0.25 2 1/36 3 2/9 4 1/17 5 1/9

Explanations

1 Outcomes: HH, HT, TH, TT. Only HH is favorable: $1/4 = 0.25$.

2 Only one outcome: $(2, 3)$. $1/36$.

3 First: $5/10$, second: $4/9$. $5/10 \times 4/9 = 20/90 = 2/9$.

4 First: $13/52$, second: $13/51$. $13/52 \times 13/51 = 169/2652 \approx 0.064$.

5 Each die: $3/6$ even. $3/6 \times 3/6 = 9/36 = 1/4$.

Section 9.7

1 25 2 10 3 12 4 5 5 1

Explanations

1 Probability: 0.5; $50 \times 0.5 = 25$.

2 Probability: $1/6$; $60 \times 1/6 = 10$.

3 Probability: $3/10$; $40 \times 0.3 = 12$.

4. Probability: $13/52 \times 12/51 \approx 0.059$; $100 \times 0.059 = 5.9 \approx 5$.

5. Probability: $1/36$; $36 \times 1/36 = 1$.

Great Job! Keep Learning with ViewMath!

Keep up the great work! Visit **viewmath.com/TX-Grade7** for free lessons, practice, and more.

Workbook

Scan Me

Step-by-Step

Scan Me

3 Practice Tests

Scan Me

5 Practice Tests

Scan Me

7 Practice Tests

Scan Me

10 Practice Tests

Scan Me

Math in 30 Days

Scan Me

Quizzes

Scan Me

Author's Final Note

I hope you enjoyed this book as much as I enjoyed writing it. Whether you are a student working throug the material, a parent supporting your child's learning, or a teacher guiding your class, I have tried to mak this book as clear and engaging as possible. I hope I have succeeded. If you have any suggestions fc improvement, please let me know. I would love to hear from you.

The accuracy of calculations is very important to me. We have done our best, but I also expect that I hav made some minor errors. Constant improvement is the name of the game. If you find any errors, please le me know. I will fix them in the next edition.

For students: Your learning journey does not end here. I have written a series of books to help you lear math. Make sure you browse through them. I especially recommend workbooks and practice tests to help yo prepare for your exams.

For parents: Thank you for investing in your child's education. I encourage you to explore the companio resources available online to help support your child outside the classroom.

For teachers: Thank you for the invaluable work you do every day. I hope this book serves as a useful resourc in your classroom. Feel free to reach out if you have suggestions or would like to discuss how best to use th book with your students.

I also enjoy reading your reviews. If you have a moment, please leave a review on where you found this boo It will help others find this book. If you have any questions or comments, please feel free to contact me at dr.nazari@ViewMath.com.

And one last thing: Remember to use online resources for additional help. I recommend using the resource on `https://ViewMath.com`. You can find video lessons, practice problems, and more. You can also use th online companion for this book to track your progress and access additional resources.

Wishing all students the best in their studies, parents every success in supporting their children, and teacher continued inspiration in their classrooms!

Dr. A. Nazari